NAILED

A Resort to Murder Mystery

I0553825

Avery Daniels

Blazing Sword
Publishing Ltd.
Colorado Springs, CO

Avery Daniels/Blazing Sword Publishing, Ltd.
Colorado Springs, CO 80907
www.blazingswordpub.com

Publisher's Note: This is a work of fiction. Names, characters, places, and incidents are products of the author's imagination or are used fictitiously. Locales and public names are sometimes used for atmospheric purposes. Any resemblance to actual people, living or dead, is entirely coincidental.

Book Layout & Design ©2013- BookDesignTemplates.com

© Cover Art, Layout, and Design by Jess/InkblotsArt

NAILED/ Avery Daniels. -- 1st ed.
ISBN 978-0-9990318-3-4

Books in the Series

ICED
NAILED
SPIKED
ARROWED

Acknowledgments

A huge "Thank You" to my critique partners, Daphne, Cynthia, and Fred who are my cheerleaders as well. I appreciate my Beta Readers more than words can tell: Rachelle M, Jeannie D, Julia D, and Jeannie H.

.

"Masks reveal in the eyes the face that lies hidden as if the mask is a dark glass mirroring your soul."

— Chloe Thurlow, Katie in Love

Chapter One

Porsche snapped the radio in the car off with a huff.

"Honestly girl, you act as though he's dumping you. He's just been working hard on getting some pristine winter photos and building up his career." Porsche burst out, unable to squelch her opinion any longer.

Porsche is my best friend since high school, currently sitting in the passenger seat on our drive through the rugged Rocky Mountains. She is a gem of a friend, a feminine bundle of brains and couture, and is an Associate Professor of History at Colorado College. I had invited Porsche to come along as a mini vacation while I attended my first Resort Management conference.

She was referring to my absentee boyfriend, Mason. I had managed to avoid talking about him in spite of her dogged efforts, until now.

"You should be a bit more enticing. A hunk like Mason may like a woman to…."

"Yeah, yeah wear more makeup and dress for him?" I'd heard it before. "He knew what he was getting before he ever pursued me." I gripped the steering wheel tighter.

Last fall had been a whirlwind with a murder in the Colorado Springs Resort where I work. I also broke up with my boyfriend Brandon at the time, and Mason Sheridan was eager to step into the role. But, he has been rather distant over the last four months since that time. We've had no real dates to speak of and he disappeared when my dad visited.

A sigh escaped me.

"Would it kill you to remind him how lucky he is to have you? Remind him he is leaving you alone around eligible rich men. Remind him how you're a desirable woman who can have any man she wants?" Porsche was describing herself not me, *clearly*.

"I don't want to talk about it, Porsche. Now, help me find the resort."

We finally entered the largest ski area in Colorado that produced several Olympic skiers. I've been skiing a grand total of three times in my life because I don't like the cold even though I love the alpine scenery. I'm definitely more the sipping hot buttered rum in the lodge great room or shopping rather than the skiing type.

The main part of Vail that visitors see has luxury condominiums, several first-class ski resorts, and the traditional cozy lodges that surround a small town teeming with a multitude of restaurants for every taste and unique shopping. As a bonus, you can catch glimpses of famous celebrities occasionally.

"At least we had clear weather for the drive up. I hope that storm blows through before we head back, or just fizzles out altogether. Turn right at the stop sign." Porsche directed.

The resort was a few streets over from the main road, giving it a secluded feel while still part of the town and convenient to the ski lifts.

"I'm just glad to attend, Chad wasn't happy he couldn't get away." I had to add. Since it was already paid for when Chad, my boss, was called into meetings with the resort owner I was the lucky runner-up to attend. "Now that we're here, I wouldn't be upset to stay a few more days if snowed in – if work pays for it that is." I couldn't help saying.

The four-day conference on Resort Management was being considered part of my training and was a big deal for me in itself. It would no doubt be a great learning experience and opportunity to network with others in my dream career field.

The premier resort hosting the conference was recently named the top resort in the state. Naturally, I'm to reconnoiter how the Bavarian-themed luxury hotel, Alpine Sun, managed the distinction and report back. We both had a specific high season but had to be creative to keep rooms full year round.

Upon my first view of the hotel, I was struck by how big the one building was, it seemed to take up an entire block.

It was like a grand Bavarian mirage in the wilderness. It all but glowed in the pervading gloom.

Alpine Sun Resort had touches of the classic white exterior with alpine timber framing and balconies fitted with window boxes for flowers in spring and summer. Aspens and evergreens surrounded the sides and back where a stream meandered past. The research I'd compiled hadn't done it justice. I felt like I'd been transported to a luxury version of a Brothers Grimm fairytale.

To the right of the entrance driveway stood a large snowman around six feet tall sporting a top hat, with a tree branch speared through its head, and a bright blood red scarf around its neck greeted me. It seemed gruesome to me and a feeling of dread washed over me.

"A slice of Germany. Feels quaint and cozy, don't you think? Hope they have a German hunk available." Porsche smiled.

"If there's one on this entire mountain, I'm sure you'll find him." Porsche attracted men with her sense of assurance and she changed boyfriends as often as her nail polish.

"With any luck." She winked. "You know me, I'll find a diversion. Don't worry about me entertaining myself."

A uniformed valet was opening my car door before I could register his presence. At the entrance, I turned and drank in the view with a deep breath tinged with the scent of pine. The snow-draped ski slopes to the one side and the quaint town on the other were idyllic.

The ominous sky, roiling gunmetal and smoky gray clouds choking out the sun, was the only blemish in the lovely tableau stretched before me. This storm system was setting up to give us a good dump of powder and the skiers would be thrilled. I wasn't too concerned. The roads were usually the main issue. Colorado is fortunate to only occasionally experience road closures.

I turned and entered the hotel. I was already taking notes about the service during check in and escorting us to our room.

Our room had plush elegant fabrics in subtle mint green and white accents on European styled furniture. No rough or basic lodge décor here. There were two chairs and a table in front of the fireplace for an evening warming up by the fire. It was a mix of classic old world style with modern comfort for an indulgent luxury feel.

"So...which of the restaurants should we try tonight? It'll determine the wow factor of my dress." Porsche asked.

My cell phone began playing the 007-Skyfall ringtone. Mason. I silenced it.

I allowed myself a few moments to conjure him in my mind. When I met him, I nicknamed him Bond Jr. because he was a playboy and his life seemed like every man's fantasy. Thus, I had intended to take the relationship with Mason slowly, but not this slowly. Mason was muscular with broad shoulders, shoulder length wavy dark brown hair, big hazel eyes with long lashes, a defined jaw, and long legs. Porsche describes him as a cross between Hugh Jackman and Aidan Turner.

Mason was in California now, playing bodyguard for a beautiful movie actress. He's prior Marine Special Forces and black belt in two martial arts. I wasn't upset...much. Can't blame a guy for working hard...much. It was back to that Bond Jr. issue and if that was what I wanted in my life.

I took a deep breath and pushed the distracting thoughts of Mason away. My nerves were a bit frazzled from the drive, racing the impending storm and I needed to unwind before talking with Mason. I looked through the in-room directory.

"They have the casual Mountain Chalet, the more western themed Ranchhand, and the upscale Maximillian's for restaurants plus the Royal Club that has live entertainment. Which do you prefer?"

"Not even taking his calls, huh?"

"He knows we're driving in the mountains and can leave a message."

"But we've arrived, we're not driving anymore." Her hands were on her hips.

"I just don't want to talk to him right now. Is that okay?" I was sharper in my reply than I intended.

She threw her hands up in surrender. "No problem."

Okay, maybe I was a little more peeved than I thought. I couldn't put exactly why I was so upset into words without sounding petty or jealous. So I was trying to avoid the topic.

We got on the wait list of the more casual choice for thirty minutes later and with only an additional ten-minute wait we were ushered into the Swiss themed restaurant within the resort, Mountain Chalet. The wall-to-wall blond wood paneling and flooring was saved from being overpowering by red with white accented table linens and other color-coordinated décor. The theme was clearly a dressy yet casual alpine.

I was immersed in the menu choices with each description a sensual tease to my imagination when every conversation stopped and all heads swiveled to the front.

A barking voice caught my attention. "What do you mean I need a reservation or wait? I'm a guest, room 321, and this is an in-hotel restaurant." The middle-aged woman had shoulder length blond hair with touches of darker honey blond in soft curls. She wore a coordinated ice blue sweater set with wide-legged navy blue pants and distinctive blue metallic pumps glared at the maître d'.

The unruffled host explained that without a reservation the wait would be about ten minutes.

"I'll wait right here. I frequent *nice restaurants* all the time, if this isn't worth the wait I'll be sure to post it on Facebook to my thousand followers." She huffed, her arms crossed.

I whispered, "So glad you called and got us a reservation."

Porsche nodded. "Me too. She must've had a bad day or a rough drive up."

We finished ordering our wine when the woman was lead past our table. She stopped and loudly greeted a thirty-something brown haired man wearing glasses with his wife and teenage boy. The boy wore a snowboarding tee shirt and jeans so I figured they were here for some famous Vail skiing.

"Christopher, good to see you again." Her barking voice carried. I was narrowing down the breed of dog her voice reminded me of to a cross between a yappy Chihuahua and the baying of a Beagle. The din of conversations and tinkling of silverware and glasses halted.

Christopher's wife opened her mouth but Christopher shook his head and gave a slight halt motion with one hand and his wife pressed her mouth into a thin line.

"Kara, you know our attorneys are used for any communication. We've nothing to say to you." His voice was strong yet controlled and clipped.

The boy's eyes were large. "You got some nerve woman." He blurted out then crossed his arms while shaking his head.

The room 321 woman continued on unfazed and sneered as she walked past another man dining with a woman. This couple seemed to be having a romantic evening because the woman was certainly dressed to seduce with a clingy red wine colored dress. The middle-aged man with graying temples glared in return. *Interesting.* I do enjoy people watching.

Conversation slowly began again.

Dinner was served and we dug in. I had ordered the Wiener Schnitzel with red cabbage and potato salad, while Porsche picked the roast duck with cucumber salad.

"How is everything tasting ladies?" Our waitress sang out, gliding to a stop at our table.

"This is so good." Porsche gushed. My mouth was full so I could only let out an appreciative "Mmmmm."

We were quiet for a while. I was enjoying watching our fellow diners as I shoveled food, as delicately as I could manage. I must've been far hungrier than I thought. I observed the couple the rude room-321 woman had glared at earlier was brought a bottle of wine.

"I didn't order this wine." The middle-aged man with graying temples said in a voice I would've expected on a teen boy whose voice hadn't fully changed yet.

"The lady at the table over there sent you this wine." The waiter indicated the loud-mouthed woman of room 321 fame seated at a table towards the back with a bottle of wine and a half glass of dark red wine. She raised one hand and wiggled her fingers in a subdued wave.

"Please send it back. I don't want anything from her." His voice may have sounded youthful, but his adamant refusal was unmistakable.

When the waiter left with the rejected bottle the woman jumped up and confronted the man. "That was rude. You can't accept a simple token gesture?" The words were loud and slurred a bit, so it sounded like a drunken Cheagle -Chihuahua/Beagle barking.

"Let's just leave, dear." The dinner companion chirped.

"Bryce, we can still be civil…" Room 321 woman began.

"Look, Kara, I've moved on. Please leave us alone." He stood and strolled out with his companion on his arm.

I caught Bryce commenting, "If I'd known she'd be here, we would have gone to Aspen. I swear." A note of desperation in his adolescent like voice.

Porsche and I exchanged a look and raised our eyebrows in unison. Kara had left quite the impact in her wake.

After dinner, sans dessert, we enjoyed a few drinks in the Royal Room. It had a men's club vibe with plush oversized chairs and loveseats scattered around, thick carpet, oil paintings and sculptures throughout, and a roaring fire in a large stone faced fireplace against one wall. The room meandered and had several sections. A local band was playing and the folksy tunes underscored the conversations all around.

Nobody from dinner was present, but conversation around us turned to the presence of a loud woman acting rude when checking in and throwing her name around as a big realtor.

"Oh, I know her alright. Kara Caine, Realtor Extraordinaire," A middle-aged woman who identified herself as Debra Graham spit out with contempt.

Ms. Graham had big brown eyes and a stick-thin frame in a gray velvet jogging suit hanging on her. Her hair was sandy brown cut in a short bob. Her voice was a caustic mix between a hiss and sizzling acid eating through metal.

"You know the kicker? I was supposedly her close friend. Until I was volunteering and coordinated a charity luncheon, but she took credit for all my work –

even got an award from the organization. Yeah, that's her." Her voice got more acidic with each word. "People think she's something until they get to know her – the real her." She nodded her head to punctuate the point. She took a drink of wine and let others share their experiences.

"We've sure had enough of her," a lady in designer slacks and matching sweater top spoke up. "My husband Wade," she nodded her head in his direction, "works for the newspaper back home and she hounds him on the message boards. She's mean and thinks she can publicly bully or something."

Wade's athletic build was clad in his forest green button-down shirt with a pistachio green sweater pullover, wearing designer glasses, and a Rolex, took a sip of his martini and clarified, "The message-boards are a public forum and all that rot, but she's mean spirited and appears to have a personal vendetta against me. I can't explain it, except maybe she gets a small bit of notoriety for her behavior." He shrugged a shoulder in nonchalant dismissal.

Porsche's eyes grew large, "Wade...Lochran? You do the editorial page for the paper, right? I didn't know there were message boards too." She had a lopsided smirk.

"The paper's trying to offer some digital content to stay competitive. The message boards get some good use such as when we have wildfires to communicate shelters and people check in as safe. But, when one person continues to use the boards for their own personal pulpit, I don't believe the public good is served.

I kept from laughing, barely. He did editorials containing primarily his opinions, but didn't see how listening to the people would serve the public good. *Okaaaaaay.* I recall he had written some controversial editorials. I vaguely recall hubbub over his staunch pro-gun and pro-life stands and the flack he received because the two views are at odds. I'm sure many expressed their opinions in the forums. So, Kara felt bold enough to take him on.

Other guests joined the conversation, mostly with stories of Kara bragging or trying to make friends in pushy and obvious ways. I couldn't help think she sounded sad or even needy. We'd had a long drive and the nice dinner provided a desire to settle into our room, so we said goodbye to the other guests.

We decided to tour the facility first and found the spacious exercise room with everything from treadmills and ellipticals to stair-climbers that I had every intention of visiting at least once during my visit. Porsche laughed at that.

We found the lovely indoor pool with a ten person hot tub to the side that looked like a Hollywood set. A few people were enjoying an evening swim and a group lounged in the Jacuzzi. I definitely wanted to enjoy a luxuriant soak during my stay.

The spa was closed so we took a brochure on the services they offered and swore we would take advantage and treat ourselves.

We stepped out on the deck adjacent to the indoor pool and took in the town lights twinkling through the trees that surrounded the resort. It was a quick look since we didn't bring our coats and the snow had begun plus the temperature was plummeting.

On the way back to the room we discussed breakfast in the morning and walking around town before I needed to check in for the conference.

Once in the room, I slipped into my coat and stepped out on the small balcony and took a deep breath. I needed a moment alone. The air was icy but invigorating. I'd needed a change of routine, a break from the job and family. The conference would be good for me.

There was no moon for the ominous sky was smothered with dark clouds. The trees surrounding the property gave the illusion of isolation. A wolf howled off to the right near the stream that I could faintly hear gurgling.

"You going to call Mason back?" Porsche joined me on the little deck.

"Never figured you for the mother role." I shot back harsher than I'd intended.

She held out my cell phone that showed I'd missed three calls from Mason, one from my boss Chad, and two from Felicia my cousin. Mason was the only one to leave a message.

"I was hoping to talk with you, but I know how difficult reception can be in the mountains. This job should be done soon. I was thinking of joining you at the resort. I'll call in the morning. Miss you."

I deleted the message. My thoughts swirled as I stared at the evergreens that were taller than the three stories of the Alpine Sun complex. Did he really miss me? He'd been traveling a good bit either for landscape photography or taking bodyguard jobs for celebrities under the guise of a playboy photographer.

It took time to build a relationship and I was feeling our getting-to-know-you stage was dying a slow death from neglect. Plus, everybody in the world saw him as footloose and very fancy-free. Could the world know him better than I? Those two thoughts combined didn't reassure me about a close relationship with him. It came down to how he wasn't giving off any vibes of being a one-woman guy anytime soon as he convinced me last fall.

Chapter Two

Despite the crisp mountain air and long day driving and settling in, I tossed and turned. No doubt the Mason dilemma was weighing heavy on me, not to mention the sense of dread. At least the foreboding had vanished. Maybe tonight I'd sleep better. Porsche was still sleeping, peaceful or not I couldn't tell. I left her a note and went down for breakfast early.

I waited at the entrance and was the first seated when the breakfast café opened. It was in the Alpine Chalet with a breakfast bar set up along one wall. The large windows along the opposite wall overlooking the ski mountain and the town were now a view into the storm that had descended on the town overnight. Snow swirled, churned, and gusted. A strong blast struck the windows, setting them rattling. A waiter started the fire in the grand stone fireplace in the center of the dining area open on both its front and back for patron's enjoyment.

The breakfast bar included standards of scrambled eggs, waffles, bagels and so forth, plus the traditional Bavarian white sausage and huge pretzel. I opted for the chef's special item for the morning, a sweet onion and herb quiche with a fruit cup.

Halfway through my first cup of coffee and shortly after my trip to pick my breakfast, I observed several staff run out the side door and congregate on a small overlook pointing into the trees surrounding the property.

Now they were bundled up in ski jackets with earmuffs and their scarves whipped around. They danced in the age-old attempt to stay warm. Could there be a moose or other striking animal below the patio of such interest? What would warrant standing out in a brutal storm?

I savored the next succulent bite, eyes closed for full appreciation, my culinary rapture was interrupted with the tramping of several feet. My eyes opened in time to see two police officers in heavy parkas go outside with the gawking group. *Oh no.* A sense of the world tilting a bit hit me. *Not again.*

"It's a body out there." The waitress with the nametag of Kylie spoke in low tones to the waiter name tagged Zachary.

"Are they sure? Could it be an animal? A dear maybe?" Zachary replied.

I took another bite of my quiche. I wasn't going to let this ruin my amazing breakfast.   Too late, it tasted flat now. The fruit cup wasn't any better. I thought about my sense of dread on the trip here and how it was gone this morning. As if there was a cosmic anxiety about the coming death. I didn't think this was an accident. *Gulp.*

"No, clearly a person.   This early and the cold temperatures overnight, it won't be pretty." They shook their heads in sympathy. They seemed too young to have that much experience with the sadder side of life. I, on the other hand, should have been too young but sadly I couldn't claim that innocence any longer.

One policeman in a parka was pointing and seeming to direct others below to the body via his hand radio. Some resort patrons gathered with excited gloved gestures and heads together.

Zachary questioned a few people who scampered inside, blowing into their hands or rubbing them together.

"No way! Seriously." Zachary's stage whisper made it to my table. It took Kylie seconds to run over to Zack with a pot of coffee still in her hands. Eventually, she returned to topping-off coffee for the few early risers.

"So, what's all the excitement about?" I asked when she reached my table.

"Well, there was this really difficult woman staying here. It seems she's dead, her body's just over the patio there. This is terrible."

"Who was it again?" Surely Kara from dinner last night wasn't the only difficult patron.

"She's some realtor who liked to throw her name around like she was somebody. She could be a good tipper if you played up to her."

"Can you describe her? I think I ran into her last night."

"You know, older, mid length styled blond hair."

Well, it could be the impatient woman last night, or any middle-aged woman from that vague description. Kylie wandered off.

When the officers came inside, apparently done directing from the patio, I had finished and assembled a breakfast to go for Porsche.

I braced myself against the frigid air and bolted out onto the patio overlook. I had to know if it was Kara from last night. The arctic blast when I opened the door made my eyes water and sucked the air from my body. Ice had already built up on the patio surface and I slid the last foot to the railing. I nearly lost my breakfast from the   unintended   ice-skating   and   accompanying adrenaline jolt.

The blowing snow made it hard to see down to the ground. I could barely make out two men below loading a person into a body bag – blue metallic shoes and navy blue pants stuck out in the white tableau.

I was positive it was the woman everybody was talking about, the divisive Kara. What a sad epitaph for her life. I squinted against an icy blast and took a brief moment to look around for splashes of blood, but there wasn't any visible, or it was already covered from blowing or drifting snow. I precariously walked back to the door, already chilled through in less than two minutes.

Chapter Three

I made my way to the spa lounge area with curved couches in a circle around the semi-open fire to catch the gossip and warm myself in the process. Porshe's breakfast was a bagel and cream cheese, so it could wait for a few moments. The fire was an open gas pit with an oblong stone base to set drinks on, with an off-white stucco flue hanging from the ceiling. It created an illusion of sitting around a campfire, in plush luxury though.

One wall was a bank of floor to ceiling windows displaying the gusting snow outside and a weak gray light, a testament to the struggle to penetrate the storm. Last night this had a peaceful view of the trees surrounding the building, this morning I couldn't see anything but snow.

"You're shivering dear. You went outside to see what the police were going on about, didn't you?" Inquired a white-haired lady in red track pants and jacket emblazoned with the Givenchy name down her sleeve.

I could only manage to nod and hold my hands out to the fire, but every head turned in my direction.

"Well, don't keep us in suspense, for heaven's sake. What's the ruckus about?"   The Givenchy clad woman pressed her garish bright red lips together.

I fought to keep my teeth from chattering long enough to say, "Woman is dead.   Don't know how she got there.   No coat.   Couldn't tell much else."   I had everyone's full attention now.

Somebody brought me a hot coffee from a nearby dispenser while another encouraged me to sit on the base around the fireplace.   I drank the black coffee and the espresso strength started to shoot warmth through my body.

Once I had drained the cup, the interrogation began.

"Was she a guest here?"

"Did you know her?"

"You're positive she is dead and not just injured?"

"How do you think she died?"

"Do you suppose she fell over the railing?"

I held up my hand to stop the onslaught.   It was like being with my Aunt Regina and the family, who I missed terribly in that moment.

"From the little I saw, no obvious signs of how she died. I don't know if she fell over.   She was being placed in a body bag, so she's definitely dead and... I think it's Kara Caine."

A fifty-something man with a few extra pounds, styled salt and pepper hair, and Hugo Boss glasses gave a start at the name. He wore an LL Bean moss green flannel button down shirt with tan Docker pants. His eyebrows drew together making his already serious frown lines deeper.

The red Givenchy woman sniffed. "Is she that loud woman who argues in public?"

I shrugged in answer. I was more interested what the others had to say. It took fifteen seconds before they were all talking again.

"She got all huffy at dinner last night I hear."

"Oh, that's nothing. She was arguing in the lobby with some man, then yelled at the desk clerk." I made a mental note to follow up on what man she was arguing with. It could be important and I will gladly share information with the police.

"Is she the one who is a troll on the newspaper message boards and carries a grudge? Because she can be mean."

"Sure, I think she's the troll. She's a realtor, isn't she? How can she sell houses with that personality?"

The man who was startled by my pronouncing Kara dead joined in, "I'm a realtor too, her clients love her. She's charismatic, charming, even funny when she wants to be."

"Hey, there are a lot of realtors here. You guys all vacation at the same time?"

"No, we have a continuing education class here. Well, it's at another hotel but I love Alpine Sun. A few of us stay here." He whipped out a business card, "Preston Pinder. Look me up if you are in the market." His lips smiled, his eyes were non-committal.

"Hey, back to the Caine woman. How can she be hot and cold, mean and charismatic all at the same time? Don't people get wise to her?"

The realtor Preston shook his head. "All I can tell you is, she really does have a following on Facebook and has people who think she is phenomenal." I mentally heard an unspoken *"but I'm not one of them."*

I looked him over a little more closely. I saw his rose-gold Cartier watch on his wrist and Prada leather loafers on his feet. Working in the Resort business you get to know the expensive styles. Success dripped from him like oil. Wonder how many houses he had to sell to maintain just the watch. My immediate impression was one of privilege and polish. I figure as competitors he and Kara were likely oil and water.

I was about to ask if anybody knew who the man Kara had argued with last night was, but a parka-clad police officer approached the group with the concierge following behind looking a bit flustered.

The concierge, Peter, rushed to speak before the officer could, "Ladies and gentlemen, we apologize for the inconvenience. The police will be taking statements regarding the unfortunate passing of a guest. If you could please wait here until he calls you into one of the spa rooms for an interview." *Interview?* Who was he kidding?

Several more guests arrived, having been directed to wait for their interviews. Peter unlocked the spa facility doors and after a few short minutes he joined us with a clipboard. He noted all our names and room numbers and then took note of who was getting their *interview*. Either it was too early for the spa to open or treatments were postponed today. I realized Porsche's bagel was going to be a tad later than I thought.

I was the third person ushered into the bright spa room with mint green and white accents and a fireplace on one wall. The massage table had been pushed against the windows that displayed the snow now turned to a brutal blizzard. I wished I had brought my clarinet because I wanted to play "A Hazy Shade of Winter". My fingers itched to fly through the chord changes to calm my nerves.

A folding table and chairs had been set up for the interrogations. The wind howled rattling the windows.

"I'm Detective Johan Larson, and you are...?" He had sandy blond hair, weary blue eyes, and a voice somewhere between Butterscotch and Caramel, sweet and warm with a touch of salt. Perfect for interrogating the resort-set. A mild voice or handshake signaled weakness to many in these circles. His voice was just masculine enough for the realtor Preston Pinders of the world to take him seriously and just sultry enough for the woman to feel flattered by his questions. He wore black corduroy pants and a thick cable knit teal sweater...and snow boots worthy of Alaska.

"Julienne LaMere." The first rule of interrogations I learned from being the prime suspect last fall, only answer the specific question, don't overshare like I do when I'm nervous. I sat back in my cold folding metal chair and scanned him up and down. *Not like that!* I was taking his measure. A detective, huh? So Vail had somebody who, at least on paper, was up to the job. That made me feel a tad better.

Detective Johan Larson took a few seconds to study me as well, no doubt looking for a speck of blood or something. He then devoted his attention to his notes and began asking questions.

"And what brings you to Alpine Sun?"

"I'm attending the resort management conference."

"How did you know Ms. Caine?"

"I didn't know her. I knew of her." I was careful to make that distinction.

He looked at me, the full force of his now intense eyes laser-focused in on me. *Gulp. Is this what a mouse feels like when a hawk is swooping in?* My heart began to drum faster.

"Another interviewee stated you shared earlier that the victim was Kara Caine. How would you know that if you didn't know Ms. Caine?" He stared at me. *The hawk is circling.*

I cleared my throat and tried for aloof. "Oh, I saw her for the first time last night at dinner and she was a bit loud when she had to wait. I found out her name was Kara Caine after dinner in the Royal Club as people were talking about her. I looked over the railing this morning when they were putting the...you know, in the body bag and noticed the metal blue shoes and navy blue pants, just like what Kara wore for dinner. That's all." I swallowed loudly and tried to slow my shallow breathing before I passed out or something equally pathetic.

Detective Larson's attention was all on me and not his notes. *Oh, goody!* I gave up on aloof and tried to look as innocent as I could - the deer in the headlights look, which may have already been on my face for all I knew.

"Where do you live, Ms. LaMere?" He was looking at his notes and jotting down private comments.

"Colorado Springs." My voice wobbled.

"Same as the victim. But you didn't know her before dinner last night?" His eyes were back to staring at me and never wavered. I wanted to look away so bad, but I felt it would be a confession or something. So I met his gaze, squirming inside all the while.

"The Springs has a population of over half a million people. No, I didn't even know of her until last night. That's not unusual you know." I bit my tongue. I caught myself wanting to chatter away.

"But, you're holding back something." He tilted his head like he was trying to get a different perspective. "Might as well just tell me so you can relax."

"It's just hearsay and speculation. I don't have any special knowledge." A defensive tone crept into my voice. My palms were sweaty and I had an overwhelming urge to fidget but I managed to meet his gaze steady. At least I think it was steady.

He leaned forward and in a conspiratorial whisper said, "I'll be careful to note it as hearsay, and since this isn't a trial I think it'll be okay."

I contributed my anxiety to the mutual suspicion with Detective Lawrence last fall. I think Lawrence fitting me for a murder-one arrest left a lasting distrust. I still didn't trust him, but I took a breath and took the plunge.

"Well okay. It seems that her ex, not sure if it's ex-husband or just ex-boyfriend, is staying here. Bryce – Caine maybe if they were married. But they didn't seem on good terms, nearly snarling at each other last night at dinner. Oh, plus there was a guy at dinner... Christopher, I think, with his wife and son. Kara stopped at their table and I overheard him clarify they must talk through their lawyers. The family clearly disliked her."

I was quiet so he could catch up with his notes that he was scribbling. He glanced up and motioned for me to continue. I told him about the former best friend in the bar who complained about her and the newspaper guy who was plagued by the victim.

"Anything else? Anything at all."

"Well, talking in the lounge out there I met a fellow realtor guy, um Preston something. He might provide you more about her 'cause he seemed to know her. But that's all I've got." I was able to breathe again.

"Where were you last night, early this morning?"

"After dinner and a stroll to tour the resort facilities, we went to the room for the night. That's my friend Porsche and I. I got up early and went down for breakfast. I was on my way to take breakfast to Porsche when I got sidetracked talking and now this." I held up the little Styrofoam box with the bagel.

"We're going to wrap this investigation up as quickly as possible. The roads have closed so you're stuck in town, but if you should go to another hotel please notify the station. Forecasts are now predicting this storm system could get much worse." The wind howled like a wolf again and the windows shook.

Things just kept getting better. Snowed in with a killer roaming the resort. I had the urge to go to the gym and practice the few self-defense moves Mason had taught me.

"Um, I noticed there wasn't any blood in the snow, at least not that I could see. How did she die? I mean, could it be an accident somehow?"

"Not much blood sometimes with this sort of wound. A nail gun to the head and then a dive over the balcony isn't looking like an accident."

My vision tunneled and my hearing went muffled. *A nail in the head and tossed out in the freezing cold. If one didn't kill her, the other probably did.*

"Ma'am, don't you faint or anything. Put your head between your knees and breathe deep." I did as he instructed and finally I recovered, embarrassed and in a hurry to escape the interview. I tried to walk in an assured and sedate manner, but I fear I near tripped over my own feet to exit my *interview.*

I entered my room to find Porsche wearing a towel and her hair wet, pacing while talking on the phone.

"I don't know why she hasn't called you back and," I shook my head *no,* "I just got out to the shower but she isn't here. Probably checking out where the conference will be…I promise I'll tell her you called…yep, okay." She hung up my phone and tossed it to me.

Okay, I was going to have to speak to Mason eventually.

"He's been calling for the last forty-five minutes, even woke me up." She had her arms crossed.

"Here's a bagel for you, I couldn't sleep so I went for breakfast early. Plus, I have two pieces of big news." I figured she would forget about Mason once she heard about the murder, or at least that was my hope.

"Okay, spill. Don't think this gets you out of dealing with Mason, girlfriend."

I walked over to the balcony doors and drew open the drapes to reveal the blizzard in all its fierce fury, and two rather large raccoons huddled in the corner of the balcony in an embrace. My throwing the drapes open had startled them and they starred up at me with big eyes and their ringed tails wrapped around them.

Porsche called the front desk before I stopped looking at the masked visitors with a goofy smile on my face. Snow had already accumulated on the little balcony but it seemed to provide some shelter for the two. I was tempted to try and slip them some food or water, but the Front desk insisted we not do exactly that. I closed the drapes part way to give them a little privacy.

"What was the other thing you wanted to tell me besides the storm raging and putting a crimp in the weekend?" She said as she began to get dressed.

"Remember that woman from dinner last night? She was found dead this morning out in the snow"

I made some in-room coffee and Porsche ate her bagel while I told her about my interesting morning.

"So, describe this detective. Don't leave anything out. Start with how old he is and what he looks like."

"Ummm, well he's probably a couple years older than us...I think. And um, he has that blond strong guy thing going for him." I was terrible at detailing what guys looked like for her. "Oh, and his voice is smooth as silk."

Her eyes were bright and she was putting on lipstick. I wondered if she could get information on the case from him, just to satisfy my curiosity of course.

"I almost feel sorry for Detective Larson when he interviews you." I smiled as she threw her hair towel at me.

My phone began ringing and Porsche crossed her arms. I answered the phone without looking.

"Oh, ummmm. Hi. Surprised to hear from you." I couldn't believe my ex-boyfriend had suddenly called.

Chapter Four

I mouthed *Brandon* to Porsche. She relocated to the bathroom and shut the door. Shortly I heard the hair dryer. Porsche had always thought Brandon was a nice guy but not the right fit for me.

"I miss you, Julienne. I don't know how this went so bad between us so fast." I ached inside. Not for anything lost, but for a relationship that was ill-fated from the start and for hurting a truly nice and decent guy.

"I thought it was a bit fast when you jumped into Tiffany Davidson's arms." I couldn't help that little barb. I wasn't that big of a person. But, he had jumped into Tiffany Davidson's arms. She was only interested in getting even with me for a perceived slight in high school. I had held Mason off thinking we still had some issues to settle between Brandon and me, but he took the easy route.

"It was fast, and died just as quickly." A few heartbeats of silence followed where I rubbed my eyes. Didn't he have amazing timing!

Through my talking with a therapist I understood I had dated Brandon because he was so very safe. My abandonment issues from my mother passing of Breast Cancer when I was just a pre-teen made me seek a person who wouldn't leave. Brandon was that sort of steadfast, stick by your side kind of guy. He was also so practical that he planned my future for me including the number of children he wanted and scrapped my dreams of traveling the world via managing resorts globally.

I rested my forehead against the balcony door, the cold on my forehead helped me focus.

"Brandon, I thought we had reached the natural end of our relationship. Remember, we hadn't been a real couple for months..." My heart was hurting. I didn't want to go through this again. Especially not when Mason and I were having some issues. "Besides, we want different things in life. You know that."

"Can we have coffee and talk. Please." It wasn't pleading, but close. I figure he needed closure, and I probably owed him that much. I didn't think for one minute we would actually work out the major differences in what we wanted in life. Besides, I had realized I didn't love him in that way, he was more a brother to me.

I watched the chaotic churning dance of the snow at the balcony door, so close my breath fogged the glass with every exhale.

"I'm out of town at a conference. It'll be a few days before I'm back. Maybe we can have coffee and talk after I get back." I wasn't just saying it because he needed some closure. Maybe we could clear the air and heal. Healing was good.

He agreed and eventually, after giving me a brief update of his life, hung up.

I glanced at the two raccoons still hunkered in a corner of the balcony. I couldn't tell where one began or ended for they were entwined for warmth. I marveled at their reaching a second-floor balcony.

Porsche entered dressed in jeans and a lovely coral sweater, makeup in place, and her game face on.

"What did Brandon want? Don't you dare tell me you're giving him a second chance." She glared.

"I think that's what he would like. But nothing has changed as far as I'm concerned." The call had dredged up emotions that were warring for attention.

She studied me for a few moments, gauging my mood or something.

"Alright enough of that. I want to get my interview over so we can get a little shopping in before your conference. It may be our only chance considering the weather."

So our first stop was Detective Johan Larson and his temporary office of interrogation in the spa.

I waited outside while Porsche was interviewed. There was a steady trickle of people arriving and waiting their turn. Most found it an inconvenience but weren't too bad about it. Porsche didn't take long.

Detective Larson walked her to the door and waved me over. I looked behind me, but he was motioning for me. *Gulp.* I was baffled. What did he want me for? Not to be whiny but being singled out by a homicide detective – well, I'd been there, done that and didn't want to go back.

"Ms. LaMere, I'd like to talk to you again." He motioned me inside but didn't sit. "I understand your conference will be starting up this afternoon. Maybe after they dismiss I could talk to you again?"

Color me shocked. "What? Why me? I mean, did I do something wrong?" I never claimed to speak eloquently. But, I would have appreciated a bit more coherence for my own sake.

"You might be able to help me. I won't have eaten and hope to wrap up interviews by the time your initial conference meeting is over. If you don't mind joining me so I can get a bite while we talk, I would appreciate it." He was serious, no twinkle in the eye at the mention of joining him for dinner.

"Um, yeah, okay. I guess so." *Think before you speak Julie. Geesh.* "Is your eating while we talk where I help you out or is there something else?" Go fish.

"When you're done just meet me at the Ranchhand restaurant on the first floor." It was the hotel's one restaurant that paid homage to being in the Rocky Mountains and the rural west with steaks, buffalo, and some wild game. "I'll be starved by then. I hope you don't mind if I eat in front of you?"

"Uh, well no I don't mind.   Seriously, you won't get anything to eat until then?"   I felt a teeny tiny bit bad for him, but I did notice he sidestepped my question.

That is how, before Porsche and I left for a little shopping, I ordered eggs and waffles from Kylie and tipped her to deliver them to the spa for Detective Larson.   I know I didn't have to, but maybe whatever his remaining questions were for me would be softened by my goodwill. Or I was trying to get better karma. *Hey, a girl could hope.*

"What was that about?" Porsche asked on our way out the front door.

"I'm not sure, he said something about helping him. It will be after he is done and discuss it over dinner so he can get something to eat."   The instant we stepped outside the blowing cold was like hitting a glacier.

"Help him. Help the police? I don't like it, you shouldn't get involved." Hmmmm. Was she remembering my past record with homicide detectives, or was she hoping this particular detective was more interested in her?

Either way, I hadn't even considered saying no, not really.

"I want to find out how he thinks I can help. I like being helpful rather than a suspect." Which was true, as far as it went. I also wanted the killer among us captured sooner rather than later. Could you blame me?

It was a short walk into town, but treacherous and bitter cold with the wind cutting through even the thickest coats. Coloradans tend to take the weather in stride, so we hadn't thought much of going into town. We had layers on and were bundled up with heavy coats, ear muffs, knit hats, sub-zero gloves and boots, and thick scarves wound around our necks. Of course, we were burning up inside the shops.

It was a surreal atmosphere, a bit frenetic energy mixed with a sense of anxiety, as the storm now seemed to worsen.

This was quickly becoming worse than the usual snowstorm. We ducked from one shop into another. Hot cider and hot chocolate were served up for brave shoppers at several stores. Word was buzzing that this could be the worst storm in a century or more. The town was bracing itself and the locals behind the counters said the grocery stores had nearly bare shelves with everyone stocking up.

We were in the last shop before we planned to return to the resort. It was a clothing boutique with unique items and jewelry.

The sales lady, who I suspected was the owner, struck up a conversation with us. "I hear there was some excitement at your place. What happened?" She had a pleasant smile, but her eyes were alive with curiosity.

"Oh, well the police are looking into something. I don't know if we're supposed to talk about it. Ongoing investigation and all." I tried to sidestep.

"I hear it was Ms. Caine found dead in the snow. What a horrible way to go." Oh yeah, small town grapevine and all. It was likely the talk of the town.

"You knew Kara then?" I said with a casual air.

"Oh, she shopped in here two days ago and seemed very pleasant. We had a good chat." Hold on one little minute. Pleasant?

Porsche and I exchanged stunned looks.

"That's a little surprising, she didn't seem in a good mood last night when I saw her. She was a bit...out of sorts. Did she share anything with you that might explain her bad mood?" I couldn't resist myself.

"She didn't mention anything, just cheery and nice as could be though."

Porsche leaned across the glass counter displaying jewelry. "I met your charming Detective Larson this morning." She smiled like a cat with cream.

The sales lady chuckled, "oh isn't he just a yummy morsel." She waggled her eyebrows at Porsche. "He isn't dating, if you were so inclined. I should give you fair warning, every single gal in a twenty-mile radius has tried to catch his eye without any luck."

I paid for the army green tee shirt with the emblem on the front of the famed 10th Mountain Division soldiers who trained nearby in mountain climbing and skiing to fight historic mountain battles in WWII. My Uncle Lars would love it. I doubted I would get out to see the statue in town to commemorate the historic troop.

All in all, our whirlwind shopping spree was successful. We found a few lovely sweaters. I found some fun and flirty earrings for my cousin Felicia. I got some Vail branded sweatshirts for Uncle Lars and cousin Loring. I found a classic apron for Aunt Regina that I knew she would love.

Porsche found some items for her family back East. They were all reduced for blizzard customers. Bonus!

We weren't the last people in town, but close as the stores were all closing up to ensure employees and owners got home safely to ride out the storm.

We couldn't get back to Alpine Sun fast enough once we gave up on shopping and followed the exact path we had walked on our return. The white landscape allowed little in the way of direction or landmarks.

The doormen rushed out to help us the last twenty feet only an hour after we had left. The ground floor was full of guests. I raised my eyebrows at the doorman helping me with my coat.

"As the storm gets worse people have been congregating around the lobby." He shrugged.

The lobby was crammed full with a hundred or so people all anxious about the storm, now predicted to be far worse than originally thought. It was like a holding pen as people restlessly milled about. The mingling of colognes and aftershaves was headache inducing.

The manager, looking haggard and drained, appeared and raised his hands for quiet. Porsche and I drew closer to the crowd to hear him.

"You may have already heard that all major roads have been closed. The radio reports extremely hazardous road conditions. We can't force anybody to stay, but we're strongly advising everyone to stay and not attempt to leave. The tourist part of town has just closed shops and only vital town services will be open. Cell service may be spotty since the networks are being overloaded. Please inform your family or friends that you may be detained due to the weather."

"Will there be enough food for all of us?"

"Will the power stay on?"

The manager held his hand up again to quiet the questions coming fast. "If the forecasts hold true, we'll have plenty of food. If the public utilities should have any outages we have backup power sources that will kick in."

"What about the murder, have the police caught the killer?"

"Yeah, are we still going to be hounded and questioned since we're stuck here?"

Really, that's what the man asked. As if that were something to worry about. *Hello,* we're stuck here with a killer lose. Bigger issue at stake.

The manager let Detective Larson join him and answer that question. "The investigation and interviews continue, but the town residents may require our attention as well for emergencies. Everyone on the local police will be pulling extra duty. There is no indication that any danger exists to any guest, just use common sense and remain cautious. Additionally, if you can provide any information or think of something after your interview, you can privately call the station or tell any officer or detective here."

"I just want to wrap up by saying we will shortly have a roster of activities posted here in the lobby to help fill your time, including children-specific activities."

Eventually, there were no further questions and the crowd began to disperse. Detective Larson made his way over to us.

"I wanted to thank you for the breakfast you arranged." He spoke to me, but he was giving Porsche his undivided attention. After a few seconds of prolonged eye contact, his ears turned red and he began an inspection of the carpet.

Porsche had claimed another victim, even the hard to catch detective. I should go easy on him, he hadn't a clue what a tornado on the back of a hurricane he had just briefly tangled with. He was toast.

I didn't know how she did it either. In high school I had studied what I thought was her technique and tried to mimic it, but it wasn't something you could be taught.

"I've got to go   . I still have many people to question. See you tonight." His caramel and butterscotch voice said as he turned tail.

I know I was supposed to meet with him, but the way he said it sounded like he meant Porsche.

Chapter Five

The beginning of the resort management conference was supposed to be registration and an informative introduction to cover the next two days. But, it turned into a practical exercise. We brainstormed ideas for activities that the conference organizers would pass along to the hotel staff. They likely had plenty of their own backup ideas, but it made us feel useful.

I suggested a masked party and the children's activity department could help with crafting masks for guests. I also thought of a popup poker night, without actual money bets to stay within the law. Prizes could be items from the gift shop. If they didn't already have casino equipment, they could improvise with conference tables and such.

It felt good to put our minds to some solutions. When the initial welcome session was finished, I made my way to the Ranchhand restaurant on the main floor, I was feeling good about doing something rather than obsess on the intensity of the storm or the amount of snow drifting.

I just stepped off the elevator when my cell phone rang. *Mason.* I took a deep breath and answered.

"Julie, thank goodness you answered." I had turned the phone off during the conference session. "It is all over the news about the blizzard. Seems you're right in the center of the worst of it."

Funny how he mentioned the news, after lunch I spent some time on the internet before I headed to the conference and Googled Mason's name. It was the only way to find out what he was doing on his bodyguard assignment. He sure didn't tell me anything, which was frustrating. Mason was all over the celebrity pages accompanying the latest Hollywood sensation starlet to the opening of her new movie, on to an awards show, and then to a tribute to a famous director. I pulled myself out of the reverie.

"It's pretty bad and cell phone service is getting unreliable. The town is hunkered in to wait out the storm. The conference is still on so I'll be busy with that." I was trying to keep my voice emotion-free.

"I was concerned, you haven't answered any of my calls. Is something wrong?" He sounded sincere, but then he always did.

But over the phone isn't what I considered authentic communication. It was too easy and non-committal to discuss what I was feeling over the phone. Not that I even fully understood what the problem was. I know seeing him all over the news with another woman ticked me off, and hurt. I didn't care if it was a job. The rest of the world didn't know it was work, they believed he was dating this actress.

I pegged him as a Don Juan playboy when I first met him. But he'd convinced me he wasn't like that, he wanted a committed relationship, was looking to settle down for the long term. I was beginning to feel duped, bordering on a fool. It didn't bother him in the least to appear to be dating this woman rather than me.

"When we're both back home, we need to talk. Not now and not over the phone." That sounded bad, and I couldn't make it sound any better and be truthful. My feeling useful from the conference went flying out into the storm and the swirling flurry of snow seemed to have settled in my stomach.

"Julie, whatever it is, I'm sure we can work through it. I'll call again to see how you're doing in the storm. I'm worried." He had no idea.

The storm was the least of any of our worries with a killer lose. But, I wasn't going to tell Mason or my family about that. We said goodbye and I stood staring off into space at the irony.

Brandon calling and wanting to resurrect our dead relationship when Mason and I need CPR for our young but failing couple status. Mason had pursued me with a single-minded attention, but as soon as I was open to and available to date him – he was busy.

Most of our time together had been family dinners with my Aunt Regina and immediate family. We barely had much time alone together and sure hadn't taken anything to a next level. I was torn, was that really something to be upset over? There was a nagging guilt telling me to be happy with what I had.

I jumped when a caramel and butterscotch voice interrupted my thoughts. "Didn't your mother ever warn you your face'll freeze with that scowl?"

Detective Larson was standing in front of me and I hadn't even noticed. His sandy blond hair looked like he'd run his hands through his hair a few times today. Wisps of hair here and there stuck out that weren't there this morning. His blue eyes looked like he needed about a week of sleep and his six foot something frame was hunched over a little.

"Oh, sorry. A phone call had me lost in thought."

"You were a million miles away, that's for sure. If you need a moment I can go get a table." Clearly, the man had food on his mind. Just then his stomach let out a rumble and I chuckled. His ears and cheeks turned crimson.

The Ranchhand Bar and Restaurant had walls of rough-hewn rocks fit together, light wood plank floors, Moose antler hanging chandeliers, and wooden plank booths and tables. The lighting was subdued, just enough to read the menu without being bright. The overall effect with the howling blowing snow outside was of an upscale cozy saloon.

We got a table tucked away and waited until a small loaf of fragrant warm bread had been placed on the table and our orders placed before I felt he was open to chatting.

"You mentioned that I could help you?" I popped a bite of the bread with butter into my mouth to keep me from babbling. "I'm surprised you would enlist an average person to assist."

He had already inhaled...or eaten a few slices and swallowed another bite coated with butter. "You're no average person. I got more information from you thus far than pretty much everyone else combined. You have a way to get people talking comfortably and you have instincts." He managed between bites of bread.

I liked this detective; he was a much better judge of people than my last experience. I may be a smidge biased, though.

"I want to help, I'm naturally curious and good at getting people to talk. But more importantly, I want a killer brought to justice and anything I can do to help that process along, I'll do." I meant it too. One of my favorite quotes was Edmund Burke's *All that is necessary for the triumph of evil is that good men do nothing.*

"We'll still be around investigating, depending upon the storm, of course. You'll be a quasi-confidential informant and a kinda-consultant. Nothing official and nothing dangerous." His voice was soft, meant only for me to hear.

I looked around to see if anybody could overhear my oh-so-confidential recruiting from the police. Nobody *appeared* to pay us any attention.

He had finished the small loaf when a waiter dropped a fresh loaf on the table and he started into that one. You'd have thought he hadn't eaten for a week. I had to admit the fresh baked aroma was intoxicating; guess I was hungrier than I thought.

He had stopped munching on another slice of bread and stared into my eyes, "You aren't to ask blatant questions, you aren't the police. You aren't to take any risks or poke around. Understood?"

"No problem," I answered but he still stared and raised an eyebrow.

"You talked to my boss, didn't you?" I sputtered.

He smiled. "Of course. I did a background check too and saw the interest in you last fall for the murder in the resort. But, those suspicions were proven unfounded. The detective then, Detective Lawrence, did a thorough look into your life and shared all that with me, so I know you pretty well. What concerns me is how you'd conducted your own investigation, had a dossier on likely suspects. None of that this time, got it?"

I nodded with a strictly business look. I'm sure the file I compiled would be laughable to this detective. But I wasn't going to explain how I was trying to provide other suspects so the horrible Detective Lawrence would investigate somebody else. Besides, I wasn't going out on a limb this time. *Nope, not me. Fingers crossed.*

He stopped to answer a few phone calls one after the other. Sounded like an officer was in the hospital and he wasn't happy about it.

Our meals came fairly quickly and for Detective Johan Larson, talk during the main course was clearly inconceivable. Not that he could have talked with how fast he devoured his meal. I should have timed him - maybe he could get a Guinness World Record.

I didn't let his speed eating stop me from enjoying my barbeque pulled pork sandwich with coleslaw, baked beans, and french fries.

Once his steak, loaded baked sweet potato, and salad were completely consumed and the plate wiped clean with more bread, he gave me my first assignment. I still didn't fully understand why he enlisted me. But I was willing to overlook that if he was.

"I'm interested in Bryce Caine and Christopher Burns at this point.   See if anybody lets slip either of their movements last night after dinner. Remember, no direct questions." He pulled cash out for his bill.

"I've got to pull a second shift at the station to free up more patrol officers. We've an officer out - injured while aiding a car that slid into a ditch when a truck slid off the road and into him. It's a mess out there when people insist on driving. Emergency vehicles are struggling too. I'll be by tomorrow, probably late morning and see if you've had any luck."

I was thinking about his specific directions. How did he think I got the information I gave him already? Gee, I asked questions, the kind anybody would. I just had to make it sound natural and common curiosity.

"Do you have any forensic evidence? You know, that I should be aware of, or keep an eye out for? I guess you've got the nail gun..." I didn't get to finish my sentence.

"How quickly you forget my instructions."

"I'm just keeping my eyes open…ah ears."

"I haven't gotten a report yet about anything found around the body or in her room. Not that I plan on telling you." He grabbed the to-go coffee he ordered and walked out leaving me to my new unofficial kinda-sorta confidential-informant duties.

Chapter Six

"How can you learn anything without some innocent questions? He doesn't understand women at all." Porsche declared.

I had to agree. People chatted, kibitzed. It's natural. That's why Porsche and I checked the new schedule of activities, on a large whiteboard in the lobby, designed to keep everyone's mind off being trapped like a caged animal. We decided to join the evening cooking class. Surely we could get some gossip going naturally.

The makeshift classroom was held in a windowless medium-sized meeting room with each six-foot table stocked with ingredients and low-tech handheld or manual equipment. A nice printed recipe card for each person to make notes on and take with them was included.

At the head of the improvised kitchen was a man in the classic tall, round, pleated, and starched white chef's hat, the toque. Chef Ryan was a thirty-something guy with blue eyes, tanned, and short brown hair with a rough edge to him. He looked like he would have been more comfortable in the Ranchhand saloon rather than teaching a cooking class.

We were to make a Chocolate Bavarian Torte that would look like the drool-worthy example in front of the class when it was done. Four layers of a chocolate cake with some cream layers between and on top. Since we were last minute additions, Porsche and I had to share and make one torte together. We were okay with that. *Wink.*

I slipped on the white apron with the Alpine Sun logo, the sun partially behind a rugged mountain with beams radiating outwards, imprinted on the front.

The best part, Chef Ryan said it would take thirty minutes for our masterpieces to bake, so the ten participants consisting of eight women and two men would get to have a drink and eat the sample torte. Which meant a perfect time to chat it up with the others. I figured Porsche would get one of the men or even Chef Ryan talking while I focused on the women.

"You'll make two rich chocolate cakes, essentially devil's food cakes. After they bake and cool, you will slice each in half with the long knife at your stations and top each layer with a whipped cream cheese frosting. The result is a decadent treat." Chef Ryan informed us and it sounded so simple. Easy for him to say.

Mixing up the dry ingredients for the cake went amazingly fast with everything already sitting out pre-measured. Porsche beat the batter with the hand whisk.

I looked around at my fellow class participants and felt good about chances of getting them talking, but would this varied group know anything about Bryce or Preston? They were a diverse group from grandmotherly types to a teen boy, designer jeans to velvet jogging sets, Rolexes to Fossil watches.

We poured the batter into the two greased and floured round cake pans. They carted away all the pans to the ovens with table numbers assigned so you got back what you mixed up. We then made the frosting and let it sit while we sat to have a slice of the provided torte with some signature hot chocolate.   After the initial exclamations of ecstasy from everyone's first taste subsided, I jumped in. I was on the job after all.

"This was a great idea to keep us busy." Everyone nodded, mouth's full. I would have to do better.

"Porsche, did you hear Kara's ex is here? I wonder if he was around and about last night? They always look at the spouse." I went for a stage whisper, just loud enough to be heard.

One of the men, a twenty-something black haired guy in an LL Bean plaid flannel shirt surprised me when he spoke up at my bait. "True. I chatted with him in the lobby this afternoon. They were married for eight years, all of which he claims were a nightmare. He seems too timid, whipped, to have killed her."

"I don't know about that, you know how they say anybody can kill if provoked or pushed far enough. He could've snapped." Said a woman in heeled boots and a Ralph Lauren sweater dress.

"I saw the two of them at dinner exchange barbs, but I didn't see him after that." I tossed into the mix to keep the talk going.

"I heard he was seen in the whirlpool with his girlfriend pretty late, like midnight." Heeled boots lady offered.

"But was Bryce seen after that by anyone?" I followed up but got shrugged shoulders or blank looks.

"Between two and four am the cop asked me about, so I guess that's the time she was killed. I would think anybody up and around at that hour would be noticed." Flannel shirt guy said.

"By whom? Everybody else is asleep at that hour." Heeled boots lady proclaimed. Although that was a good point, I was with the flannel guy. Somebody had to have seen something.

"Unless somebody was...ummmm, leaving one room and going to their own." I tossed out to keep the conversation going. If somebody had a one-night fling and was walking back to their own room at that hour, they could have seen a person and thought they were doing the same. But how could we ever figure that out? Surely, after the news and interview with the cops that information would have come out.

This was going nowhere. I hated to waste the time.

"I heard Kara got into an argument in the lobby. I wonder who that was with." It was worth a shot.

"Oh, that was the real estate agent guy.   I was there. They were arguing over a deal that went bad and that Preston fellow said she owed him the earnest money and an apology." Replied a grandmotherly looking woman with too much blush and too bright of red lipstick. I couldn't help but wonder what brought her to ski country. I couldn't see her on skis, but I could be wrong.

Well, at least there was that piece of information.

Porsche jumped into the fray, "What about that Chris guy? At dinner we heard him and his wife tell Kara to talk to their lawyer. I think they sued her."

"I heard somebody say they were suing her for selling them a house when she knew advance plans of a major road going through the neighborhood.   They had to move after only three years. I admit I'd sue her butt, too." The sweet looking senior lady shared. Okay, maybe she was more of a spitfire than I initially thought.

"I wonder where he was after dinner?" Nobody seemed to know where lawsuit-Chris had been.

The cakes came back and the warm chocolate smell lifted my mood automatically. We commenced to remove them from the pans and very carefully cut them in half, then layer with frosting.   After covering the top, we shaved chocolate curls for the final decorative touch on top. I didn't know how we would eat it after indulging already, but we packaged it up in the provided cardboard box with the logo on top.

Once we left the meeting room with our Chocolate Belgium Torte, we returned to our room and I stuck the torte in the little refrigerator.

"I liked the class. I'm glad we got at least some information, but even if we hadn't gotten those tidbits I had fun. I'll have to make this at home." I shared. I was proud of our effort and thought I would make this for the next family dinner and surprise Aunt Regina.

"Hey, looks like we have a message. The hotel phone is blinking its red light." Porsche dialed the message retrieval number and listened. "There is something waiting at the desk for you." She called down to reception. "They're sending somebody up with something for you."

I hadn't a clue what it could be, but after a few minutes, there was a knock at the door.

"Miss Julienne LaMere, these are for you from our gift shop, we have an onsite floral greenhouse." He handed me a bouquet of flowers with white lilies, lavender daisies, some white asters, a sprinkling of purple lilies, purple button poms, and greenery all in a royal purple vase. I tipped him and sat the flowers down. They were lovely and produced a soft scent that no doubt would perfume the room.

I stared at the flowers like they were a Trojan horse, all lovely and innocent while hiding something dangerous. I took a deep breath and removed the card.

"Ma bichette, I'm thinking of you. Stay safe. Wish we were together. We will have more time together soon. I promise. Mason." It was a nice - lovely gesture but made my heart ache a little. My heart squeezed and I had a hard

time breathing and my eyes swam. I blinked away the tears and forced a deep breath.

Porsche looked over my shoulder. "Ahhhh, he still calls you little doe." I didn't want to discuss this with Porsche. I was right, the beautiful flowers were an emotional ambush and I already knew what Porsche would say. At least I thought I did. I honestly didn't know what I was feeling. Was I jealous of his time with an actress? Was I being needy or insecure and placing unrealistic demands on him? I was still working on what I felt. I put the card back and faced my dear friend.

"Right now I'm concerned at the lack of progress we made this evening."

"It wasn't a total bust, we discovered it was the realtor guy who had the argument with Kara. We know that Bryce was seen around midnight at the hot tub."

"But at this rate, we'll be picking up a few bread crumbs and get nowhere. Plus, I'll be in the conference most of tomorrow." I huffed.

"You can pump that crowd, particularly during your luncheon time and between workshops. You may find a wealth of information. I can check out gossip all day. Besides, I'm hoping to interview that cop again"

"You were questioned already today." Porsche just raised her eyebrows at me. Oh, she had a guy in her sights. I chuckled.

"Still, I think we need a plan of attack for gathering information."

"Too bad we don't have the Baker Street Irregulars like Sherlock," Porsche said as she threw herself on her bed.

Eureka.

"That's just what we need, a network of eyes and ears to help gather information. But who can we trust?"

She propped herself up on her elbows, "What? You can't actually think we can create a network of complete strangers and possible suspects."

"Well...what if we handpicked a few of the staff who have worked here for a while, so they are trustworthy, and asked them to share information they overhear of the whereabouts of the few names on our suspect list?"

"You think an employee couldn't have killed her?" She challenged.

"I don't think so, they'd have no motive. She seemed to be new to the resort. Plus, any information they gather will no doubt be verified by Detective Larson. It isn't like we're asking for physical evidence, just hearsay which is just what Larson was trying to get from me." It wasn't the best argument, I grant you that. Still, I thought it was reasonable.

"I guess it could work. It would cover more ground. But, why would they tell us anything they hear?"

"I think the staff probably knows I had dinner with Larson, and if you start pursuing him it will look like we are working with him. We can hint at doing some legwork for him while his time is being taken with the storm issues."

We compiled who we would approach in the morning to help us out. I would find Kyle and Zack from breakfast and enlist them.   Porsche had a doorman she could talk to about helping.

"Feel better with our Resort Irregulars plan?"

"Yes, actually I do."   I just hoped it would work.   In a way, I had the same setup with my neighbors last fall as they each funneled information to me about the pastor's murder.

Before bed I texted Mason.   *"Got your flowers. They're beautiful."*

Mason: *"Thinking of you. Don't let time apart get you down."*

"Up early –good night."

Mason: *"See you in my dreams. xoxo"*

A heavy sigh escaped me. He seemed like the perfect boyfriend, yet I was in turmoil. I closed my eyes hoping for dreamless sleep.

Chapter Seven

My sleep was plagued with strange dreams of raccoons staring at me through the window while a killer tried to break into my room. I woke up feeling like I'd worked all night and then was slapped with the smell of a bouquet of flowers from Mason. Argggg. I was in a fog and I crept around in slow motion letting Porsche sleep. A hot shower helped clear the last bits of the dream away.

I had just enough time to talk with Kylie and Zack before going into my resort management conference for most of the day. Porsche was just up and making coffee in the single serve in-room coffee maker by the time I was rushing out the door. I didn't see Kylie anywhere in the breakfast café and Zack was swamped. I promised I would track them down when I had enough free time.

I went to the conference main meeting room and claimed a seat in the second row. The large room had rich polished woods from the tables to the paneling, along with comfortable padded seats and stylish lighting. Nice carpet helped muffle noise from scraping chairs and foot traffic. The setup was a basic classroom setting with rows of tables and chairs with a middle aisle. The wood frames with gold fabric were a stylish but sound absorbing removable panels between rooms. They would likely remove these panels between several rooms to accommodate our luncheon.

In spite of the warm fabrics and polished woods, it felt like being in a box inside an isolated hotel. She recognized a tickle of claustrophobia that even the few multi-paned windows with limited visibility into a frozen snowy white world didn't alleviate.

More attendees were filtering in and the tables were slowly filling up. I found fresh coffee and breakfast goodies at the back of the room. I could have let out a cheer at the site, but it would be anemic at best. I also discovered Kylie bringing in a second tray of breakfast items.

"Oh, hi ma'am. At least all you conference attendees will be busy during the day. The worst thing about this blizzard is how everyone will get antsy and bored. Well, I guess the worst thing is being stuck, but you know." Her perky youthful voice was almost too much for me after my troubled sleep. The noise level had crept louder and I felt I was talking too low to be heard by others.

"Kylie, I needed to chat with you." I strolled over to a quiet corner out of hearing from others who were milling around.

"Ma'am, is there a problem? "

"I don't know if you are aware of my meeting with Detective Larson last night." I left it as not quite a question.

Her mouth quirked up into a half smile. "Oh, the staff are all talking about it alright. We didn't think you were his type."

"I don't know about that, but he's going to be rather busy with public safety demands with the blizzard. He asked me to assist him by keeping my eyes and ears open for any information on a few people regarding the other night." I kept my voice to a confidential level.

Her eyebrows went up.

"I was hoping to enlist your help for the next few days. We're interested in certain people and their whereabouts that night and early morning. Anything you might pick up on in a conversation. Do you think you could tell me and I can compile the information and give it to Detective Larson?"

I held my breath while she considered. It seemed like ages, but her eyebrows finally settled down to normal. She puckered her mouth in that old *hmmmmm, I don't know about this* expression.

"Let me think about it and I'll get back to you at lunchtime." She spun around and went back to the refreshment tables, grabbed two empty carafes and left to refill them.

I loaded a plate with the newly arrived dish labeled "Baked French Toast Bagel with a maple glaze" and some black coffee. I sat in my seat and ate the small bites of baked and coated bagel. I was fretting over whether the

Resort Irregulars idea was going to blow up in my face and barely caught the announcement.

"...total snowfall from yesterday until midnight has been twenty-two inches. It continues to snow, but the temperatures are expected to drop making it too cold to snow by this afternoon. Predictions include increased winds as well. So folks, we're here for a while. They can't get the roads cleared with the blowing snow and dropping temperatures would be deadly if a car gets stuck on the road."

"Not to mention the danger of a car getting struck by a snow plow when they come through." An audience member added.

The woman sitting next to me leaned over, "I'm from New Mexico, is this typical weather?" I estimated she was in her late forties. She had shoulder length golden styled hair, basic makeup, manicured nails, and wore a dress with a matching blazer that gave the impression of feminine yet professional. Her voice was measured and assured.

"Not particularly. But the Rocky Mountains certainly get their share of snow and storms. This weather system is a combination of factors." I was used to hearing snowstorm horror stories growing up in the state. People still talk about the Christmas blizzard of 1982.

"On the local weather, they called it an Albuquerque Low. I was surprised by that name. I wanted to defend New Mexico's honor somehow." She smiled to soften her words and I suspected she was trying to strike up conversation more than anything.

"It's only named that because the storm, a low-pressure system, swings down to Albuquerque area then directly up to us in Colorado. Those storms tend to pack a wallop with a lot of snow. Nothing against your state, I promise." I hadn't seen this lady around before. I couldn't help but consider her as a potential source of information, for both my career and my murder suspects.

I held my hand out, "Julienne, management trainee from Colorado Springs." She shook my hand and a toothy grin blossomed.

"Tammy, assistant manager from Santa Fe." We exchanged cards.

I sucked in my breath. Dawn's Waterfall Spa Resort was a smaller resort but consistently received perfect ratings from guests and had been featured in a hotel management magazine for their customer satisfaction. Plus, the property sounded beautiful, peaceful, and rejuvenating with their yoga and exercise classes. I wanted to visit there someday rather than the large Santa Fe resort with golf and a casino.

"I read the article on your property. I have dreamt of staying there when I get to Santa Fe."

"And I want to visit your sprawling resort as well." She crooned with enthusiasm.

"How long have you been in resort management?"

"Oh goodness, I hate to give my age away, but a good twenty years now."

I had a good feeling about Tammy, she had an air of competency and quiet authority that was reassuring. She was a successful woman in resort management and probably had seen many changes in the industry over the years that I could learn from.

People were moving to the workshop they wanted for the first session of the day. I was headed to the Hospitality Computer Applications session but didn't want to stop chatting with Tammy.

"Would you mind if we sat together at lunch? I would love to discuss this career path with you." There, I invited myself. You always hear about finding a mentor, but how to go about it isn't covered as much. I hope I didn't seem like I only wanted to pick her brain.

"And I'd love to get some insights from a younger generation." She smiled in return and I did a little happy dance internally.

Two morning sessions done and we were all back in the large room set up with round tables that crammed ten people together. My sessions had been chocked full of information. But my rough night and emotional strains of the last day had me with a sluggish mind.

I spotted Tammy and joined her at a table close to the speaker's podium. Lunch was a buffet and Kylie and Zack both were tending the food setup. The buffet was at the back of the room making it less convenient to talk to Kylie and Zack as the crowds descended.

I excused myself from Tammy and rushed up to Kylie.

"Can we talk before lunch gets underway?"

"I have to be quick, they're keeping us busy since we're stuck here too." She didn't sound happy.

I followed her to the end of the buffet table as she got the meat cutting station ready.

"Did you think about our discussion?" I jumped in, she would either help or not. If she said no I hoped she wouldn't tell Detective Larson. Porsche said she would corner – I mean meet with – Larson and share what information we gathered last night. Maybe he would go easy on us if she were dazzling him.

"I saw your friend with Larson this morning. I guess you guys are helping him. I'll pass along anything I hear." I was equal parts relieved and excited.

Guess Porsche was charming the detective as she planned. The man didn't have a chance. I tried not to smile or jump like a kid for Porsche. No happy dance in front of everyone, it's rude after a murder. I felt Porsche going for a more serious man was a good sign.

Chapter Eight

"I'm going to ask Zack to help as well, but I'll have to catch him after lunch." Kylie continued.

I caught sight of Zack running dishes to the table on a cart and off again to the kitchens. I took a look around, nobody was paying any attention to us. Good.

"I can fill him in. Tell me the names you want us to listen for info on." She was rushed so I quickly ran down my list with ex-hubby Bryce and lawsuit-Chris at the top. I know Detective Larson was only interested in the Bryce and Chris, but I was saving him the trouble of adding to the list later. *I'm doing him a favor, really. I'm thoughtful that way. See my halo?*

"Either Zack or I will come by your room later and tell you what we have from today. What time should we meet?" She was shuffling items to look busy since she finished the meat station. She glanced around a few times, her eyes following people.

"Would ten be too late? I know you have long days starting with breakfast rush."

"We aren't allowed in a guest's rooms so be ready to open the door and let us in so we aren't seen." The din of people talking over each other was growing louder, even some raucous laughter contributed to the noise.

Back at my table I tried to breathe deep and relax, but I kept watching for Zack. He was doing the legwork of the crew and once the buffet table was open, conference attendees descended in a wave. I saw Kylie pull him aside to talk. I lost sight of them though and didn't witness his reaction.

Between bites of Chicken Cordon Bleu, I looked for an opening to steer the conversation. I almost hated to spoil enjoyment of my lunch with thoughts of violence.

Talk at the table was focused on the weather and concerns on being stuck into next week. I couldn't imagine the weather staying bad for that long; Colorado's storms usually hit and ran letting roads clear before another storm and thus providing a reprieve.

"What about the murder, won't we have to stay for the investigation of the murder?" I jumped at my opportunity, hoping to turn the conversation. The police couldn't actually hold us to investigate, but if I was very lucky it would at least get the conversation flowing in the direction of the murder.

"I don't think they can force us to stay. It just doesn't seem real though, a murder in such a reputable establishment." Said a man in his fifties who wore a business suit and an aloof aura. Most attendees were dressed in nice jeans or khakis and sweaters. It seemed what he really meant was murder didn't happen among the wealthy and he was shocked, just shocked. I wanted to snort out loud at his naiveté and pretension. I held back rather than embarrass myself.

"I'd have thought somebody would've seen or known something and an arrest made by now." I resisted telling them to work with me and talk already.

"Oh, I think the problem is who to focus on, there are a plethora of suspects. You either loved Kara or hated her from what I've heard." I wanted to kiss the matronly woman with curly graying hair who offered up that gem. She wore impeccable jeans with a seam ironed down the front. Her voice was melodic but hinted at steel underneath.

I nodded my head in agreement and looked at the others while taking the last bite of my chicken. I turned my coffee mug right side up to indicate I wanted coffee now that I'd finished the entrée.

One woman, Nancy I think, leaned in and said, "Well, the *friend* that she betrayed sure has plenty to say about her. I listened for *fifteen minutes* as she ranted about what a horrible person she'd been. She has an abundance of pent-up anger. I have to wonder where she was when the Caine woman went flying down three stories to her death."

"I think she closed the bar that night getting plenty polluted from what I heard. That was around two. I also heard she left alone, so no alibi for her." The matronly woman replied.

The horses were out of the gate, so to speak. They were nearly talking over each other and I struggled to keep up and not to miss anything. I didn't want to take notes in front of them, so I would have to jot this down after lunch.

"What about that self-righteous newspaper guy? After a few drinks, he had some choice words about how evil that woman was and some vendetta he swears she had against him. Him being so morally upstanding, I was surprised at his language."

"Oh, his wife'll be an alibi, you can count on that."

"Sure, but where was he? He left the bar about midnight."

"I heard both he and his wife were at the Jacuzzi for a little while, but that doesn't count for the critical two through four a.m. hours."

"You heard about that other realtor arguing with her, didn't you? Wonder where he was?"

"Oh, I hear somebody saw him in the exercise room jogging on the treadmill around ten-thirty last night."

"His wife'll probably be his alibi too, no matter what."

Tammy leaned over and whispered, "You seem particularly interested in the murder."

My mouth went dry and I chocked. This time I didn't have to work for the deer-in-headlights-look, I could feel my eyes were big against my will. Was I that obvious?

"Oh, I assisted in a murder investigation that took place last fall at my home resort." I didn't feel it necessary to share that I had been the main suspect and the police didn't bless my poking around.

"Really? You assisted the police?" Surprise evident from her raised eyebrows to her cocked head.

"Who knows, somebody may know an important tidbit and they don't realize it. I like to help the police whenever I can." *Hey, I am helpful.* I held my breath to see if she accepted my explanation.

Tammy's mouth gave way to the slightest smile, just a fraction more than Mona Lisa succumbed to, but not by much.

"I'll keep my ears tuned to the chatter, then. What should I pay attention to?" Her eyes had a spark of... mischief. This was a surprise development.

I shared the persons of interest. "Nothing more than listen and report." I felt duty-bound to clarify. She winked, *actually winked at me.*

"This gives me a purpose that is a bit more active. I love to help as well." That shadow of a smile again accompanied by a definite twinkle in her eyes. Tammy was a gal after my own heart.

I looked around again and saw Zack at the buffet table trying to catch my eye.

"I'm getting some dessert, can I get you any?" Tammy declined and I headed for the Zack.

"I'm on board," he said once I was close. "I want to help get this nightmare over. Kylie gave me the names."

I looked over the dessert as if there was a question in my mind what I would get. "I appreciate the extra ears, just keep this a secret or it won't work."

He glanced around again and cleared his throat as somebody headed our direction.

I grabbed the Crème Brûlée took it back to the table to devour. My coffee cup was full and the bold rich aroma mingled with the vanilla and caramelized sugar crust of the Crème Brûlée to make my mouth water. I was going to need that coffee. I would be fighting to stay awake in the afternoon workshops.

I was the last person at my table, finishing up my dessert. I tossed my napkin on the table and headed to the workshop covering multiple-day events and Tammy had gone to her own session.

I was weary by the time the first day of the conference finally finished. I had absorbed so much information and taken copious notes to share with Chad. I was looking forward to a swim and Jacuzzi time before dinner to relax a bit if Porsche could wait that long for dinner.

I was walking with the crowd of fellow conference attendees to the elevators and staircase, moving like cattle coming out of a holding pen, jostling each other, moving around bottlenecks in the flow, and ready to trample anything blocking our path.

My mind was scattered and wandering to the thought of a cocktail when I caught sight of Detective Larson observing the crowd. Our eyes met and he slightly nodded in the general direction of the spa and walked in that direction. I struggled like a Salmon going upstream to leave the rushing river of attendees.

I didn't see Larson anywhere until I ventured into the spa, now busy with people getting seaweed wraps or deep tissue massage. The room used for the interrogations, oh sorry – *interviews*, was open and Larson waved me in, I shut the door for privacy. He was wearing sky blue ski pants and a heavy sweater, the matching ski jacket was draped over the back of his metal chair. A bolt of apprehension shot through me, *could he know about my merry band of helpers?*

"I…ahhh…you wanted to talk to me?" I began.

"The storm has pulled my attention so I hope you've made some progress today. I already got your news of last night's cooking class from Porsche." I studied his face and he looked the same as yesterday, except around the eyes where fatigue was making his crows feet more pronounced and dark circles had begun.

The thought flit through my mind that he wasn't a pretty boy like Porsche typically dated. He was more the self-assured, mature, and responsible man that she had never shown an interest in before. Oh, sure he was good looking in a more rugged woodsman way. I took it as a good sign she was gravitating towards Detective Larson.

"Well, the most fruitful conversations were during lunch." I opened my notebook to my section for the investigation.

"Folks are noticing Debra Graham has a lot of pent-up anger toward Ms. Caine and she closed the bar that night around two a.m. and left alone. The editor guy, Wade I think, he was ranting about Ms. Caine having a vendetta against him and left the bar that night around midnight with his wife and was then seen at the Jacuzzi but no idea about the two-to-four time frame." I took a breath.

"Realtor guy Preston was seen in the exercise room after the argument in the lobby with Kara. But nothing mentioned today on Bryce or Chris Burns." I closed my notes and looked up.

"Interesting how so far nobody has an alibi except that provided by a significant other. So, nobody is really off my list. I do need to know more about Bryce and Chris though."

"Well, I have tonight still. I plan on dinner and some time at the pool."

"They have opened a cash bar at the pool in the interest of keeping guests happy. Maybe that will loosen some tongues to chat with you."

"Well, I should get going then." I stood to do just that. I had to keep moving before I ran out of steam.

"I was hoping to ask you about your friend, Ms. Abrams." He stared at his hands sitting folded on the card table. He finally looked up. "She, ummm, seems interested in me. I just wondered...." He seemed to struggle with finding his words, or maybe the right words. "If she could actually be interested in, you know, a cop?"

Oh crap. I didn't want to be in the middle of this. "She knows her own mind, and I think she considers a man on more than just their job or career choices." I wasn't going to tell him she tends to have short-lived relationships, so if he just wanted to have some fun, she was his girl. *Nope, not my place.* But I didn't want him to approach her without understanding her.

"I, ahhhh, well, I should mention....you know she's leaving when this weekend is over and the roads open again. I just mean to say, enjoy her company while she's here."

His face was serious as he nodded, "Right, of course." *Okay then.* He never showed the slightest joy over spending time with Porsche, most guys were wondering how they got so lucky. Let's face it, Porsche was a feminine storm that left men with silly grins on their faces even after she was long gone.

"I'm having dinner with her tonight, then I'll be doing another few hours of a shift. You're welcome to join us." Now his eyes seemed to plead with me. *Was he afraid of my best friend?*

"Johan, I wouldn't dream of being a third wheel and interfering in the two of you having time to get to know each other." I wasn't about to coddle the strong homicide detective due to meet a velvet tigress. *What doesn't kill you...*

Chapter Nine

I was tired but wanted to get more done on the murder since my day had been consumed with the conference. As informative and sometimes overwhelming as the conference was, I had to take advantage of every hour outside the workshops and lectures if I was to be any help.

I waded through the flurry of bustle in the lobby to study the ever-changing event board. It was chocked full of activities for every age. There were children racing around, people seated chatting with old or new friends, others checking the board, many in line for one of the restaurants, and still others rushing to the next thing to do. It was like an island of activity and noise afloat in the midst of a blizzard.

There was a listing on the board for Monday night, the day after the conference was finished, for something labeled "Fasching" with the explanation below of "A German Carnival celebration" and it noted the youth would create decorative masks for the party. A little quiver of excitement shot through me to see my suggestion implemented with the resort's own Bavarian theme. I still held out hope that by that time the snow and investigation might be resolved and the Fasching wouldn't be necessary.

I entered the peace and comparative tranquility of my room to find Porsche getting ready for her dinner date with the detective. The scent of Mason's flowers permeated every corner now and promised to be an emotional reminder of him rather than allowing me some time to process.

"Okay, I didn't pack enough dresses. Which do you like? This or this?" She held up a cobalt blue knit sheath dress that would turn Larson into a nervous bunny and a burgundy red colored off the shoulder sweater dress that was pure seduction.

"Depends on the effect you're going for?" I hated giving wardrobe advice. I was no good with such emotionally charged decisions. Cousin Felicia tended to dress me for important occasions, claiming I was too stuffy.

"I want him to like me, you know, enough for another date. I like him, Julie." There was something in her voice that made me study her closer. She had less makeup than usual, her hair was down and flowing. "So I'm going for...I don't know. Dressy for our first date but not vamp on the make."

She wants a second or third date in the few days we have here? "Well, the red is out, that is femme fatale all the way." I casually glanced her way. "You do remember we are only here for a short few days, right?"

"Ah ha." She held up one earring after another from her stash and evaluated the effect in the mirror. "None of my earrings will work. Can I borrow your button pearl studs?"

Wow, she never ever borrowed anything of mine. Nobody did, actually. "I guess, sure." I dug them out of my suitcase. They were the only jewelry I consistently took on any trip.

She finally settled on my simple pearl choker necklace with matching earrings and my matching pearl strap watch. I don't think I had ever seen her so nervous.

"I'm glad you're having dinner with Detective Larson, he seems like a good guy." And he was a nice guy as far as I could tell. I was getting uncomfortable with her fussing.

She turned from the mirror and faced me. "Julie, please tell me what's going on with you and Mason. I'm on your side, if I need to kick his butt for you, I will. Just talk to me." She sat down on her bed and I sat on mine facing her.

I couldn't avoid this any longer. "I'll try to find the words. I know what it's not. It's not about any abandonment issues resulting from my mother's death. I've been working on that." I shrugged.

"Are you feeling neglected with how busy he's been?"

"That's only part of it. Yes, he hasn't been around much for us to really spend time together, but...well. It's as if he went from pursuing me to cold feet in an instant...and then there's the bodyguard jobs he's still taking. That really....gets under my skin." I avoided her eyes. This was difficult to talk about even with her. Maybe the emotions were still too raw. I began to fidget.

"That's what he's doing in California, bodyguard? What bothers you about that? It's a job, right?" And there was the rub, I was upset over one of his jobs. How could I be upset over that?

"He's with that actress from the new blockbuster hit. She has a stalker apparently. It's not her, it's not that he is working. It's....it's just..." I sputtered to a stop. It seemed petty, which made me feel guilty for feeling upset in the first place. I was twisting a strand of hair around my index finger.

"Do you think he's being unfaithful?"

"No, but how would I know? Everybody thinks they're a couple and not a bodyguard accompanying her around. The papers have them as the hot new couple, the celebrity photographer with the starlet. Aren't they the hottest couple around?" My voice had a hardened edge now.

"I think we have what's upset you. Does everyone think they're a couple, really?" Her voice had a touch of surprise.

I took my phone and opened a celebrity news website and brought up the news from earlier today. The headlines proclaimed the hot new romance was progressing with pictures of the happy couple attending an awards show. Mason looked like Bond Jr. all over again in my mind.

"Wow, I had no idea. Clearly, you've been following the gossip." She handed my phone back. "Put into words what angers you the most about this."

"He hasn't changed his bachelor ways....his gallivanting playboy image...even though....he....he said he was looking for long-term and to settle down. But this! This is the playboy he said he wasn't." I took a breath and let out the last words with a tear sliding down my cheek, "Am I just that gullible and stupid?"

~ ~ ~ ~ ~

Porsche was a few minutes late for her dinner because she made sure I was feeling better and not blaming myself. She got me laughing with outrageous punishments for Mason she would exact on him. My favorite was how she would tie him to a chair and force him to watch a marathon of chick flicks for his sensitivity training. I am blessed to have her as a friend.

I phoned and made a dinner reservation at the Ranchhand again so Porsche could enjoy her dinner without needing to invite me to join them in the elegant restaurant and I wasn't in the mood for the Moutain Chalet. The hostess gave me a time of twenty-five minutes. Just enough time to quickly talk to Aunt Regina before going down for dinner. I had texted her I was fine at the resort when I learned the roads were closed. I knew she would pass the information along to everyone else. But it would sound good to hear her voice.

"Oh Julie, thanks for calling. I was hoping to talk to you." Aunt Regina always made me feel good.

"I have a few minutes before my timeslot to get dinner so I wanted to chat with you."

I told her about the blowing snow and bad accidents on the treacherous roads, shared about my first day in the conference, then covered the efforts to keep everyone busy. I finished with the pièce de résistance – making the Bavarian Crème Torte last night. She was dutifully impressed. We hung up and I changed into more comfortable jeans and sweater.

I received a text from Mason that included a photo of the awards show he attended showing him in front of the red carpet. He said, "Wish you were here." How could a girl compete with that? He got to live a life that most people only dream about and it was his job. I didn't reply.

The winds were still treacherous and thus the wind chill was deadly cold outside in spite of the snow having stopped. I checked on the huddled raccoons on the balcony. I think they had shifted around a little bit, but they didn't seem very active. A pair of eyes opened in the mass of fur and peeked at me, glowing in the reflected light from the room.

I couldn't stand not helping them any longer. I grabbed an extra blanket and ice cube tongs then opened the sliding door. Gusts blew swirling snow inside, but this balcony was somehow sheltered from the brunt of the wind. I opened up the blanket and crouched down, with the tongs I reached one corner over and then tossed the rest. It landed on the pair, and I saw a little movement underneath, but they stayed. I closed the door and danced around to warm up.

At worst I would owe the resort for a blanket. With my conscience satisfied, I left for dinner.

I was ushered into the Ranchhand without any further wait and congratulated myself for getting into the habit of getting a reservation ahead of time. Even though I had just eaten there last night, I saw several items on the menu I wanted to try. The wood plank floors and walls seemed to reverberate with the conversations of a packed to capacity space and the myriad of foods smells mixed.

I choose the Chicken Pot Pie this time with a side salad and a hot buttered rum drink. I needed to relax before my next investigation idea.

I scanned the crowd, craning my neck occasionally, even stood at one point. The only one of my suspects present was Bryce. He was warming a seat at the western style bar and nursing a mixed drink. No sign of his girlfriend. It appeared that the gossip was correct and she had left. I guess that cleared her.

I hadn't thought of it before, but her leaving could have made Bryce mad enough, after all the years of Kara's emotional battering, to snap and get even. I know it seemed he was too beaten down, but that could have been part of what made him break. She sabotaged a new relationship and wouldn't let him move on...in front of a restaurant full of people. Of the things that people snapped over, I figured that was up there in the top ten.

I got my drink and salad plopped on my table, the waiter too busy to chat. I watched Bryce as I forked the salad into my mouth. He was lethargic, almost like he was in shock...

or maybe he'd had too much to drink. He finally raised the glass to his lips and took a swig, then returned to his original slumped over position.

It was clear he wasn't going to offer me much more than a depressed or sullen routine. Which could be guilt or something as a result of killing somebody. I couldn't imagine, but I would think the guilt would kick in and some might turn to booze. I glanced at him occasionally just to check if he had moved or was showing signs of life. He had a fresh drink delivered was about it. My chicken pot pie was plopped down and the salad dish vanished as my hit-and-run waiter ran past.

Dinner was great even if the wait staff was run ragged. I ate the last morsels and raised my credit card in one hand, my waiter sped past snatching it out of my hand and in five minutes the slip for me to sign was at my elbow with a pen. I squeezed past people on my way out, my plan was to check out the game room for any gossip among the youth, then relax a little in the Jacuzzi before I expected the visit from Kylie or Zack.

I walked into the game room and entered another dimension. It had dark red and blue walls with a few game related posters, and a wall of video games, including the classic Mario, Pacman, and Galaga. There was a foosball table, air hockey, classic skeeball, basketball SuperShot, a couple of pinball machines, a Guitar Hero, and a dance machine. Off to the side were two billiard tables, seemingly aloof and set apart from the cacophony of sensory overload machines.

I had gone from the noise of a busy restaurant to the lights and loud sound effects of an arcade where time became irrelevant. In some respects, it was like gambling machines without the payout. From a purely resort amenity aspect, I was impressed and made a mental note to share this youth game room concept with Chad for more on-site family-friendly activities.

I waded into the crowd of young faces gathered in groupings around each machine or game. It became obvious that I wouldn't get any gossip among the groups playing, so I played the dance machine (and did pretty good if I do say so myself) and a pinball machine to look like I was like everybody.

After a few games, I joined a group standing around checking their cell phones and talking. I hoped to get them gossiping since they weren't obsessively playing. I found myself at a loss how to get these teens to talk, so I punted.

"Not interested in these games? I guess they get old after a day or two." Three teen boys looked up from their phones.

"No, texting my fam." The brown-haired boy who looked a little like a young pop singer said. He glanced up at me and did a double take, giving me a shy smile.

"Yeah, I'm chatting with my squad, too." The freckled boy added.

I took a guess they were texting their friends. Somehow, I had grown up and I no longer could relate to the teenagers of today. When did that happen?

"I already let my friends know about the storm and being stuck here. I hope they find who killed that woman quick." I gave up on trying to be smooth, I was okay with being clumsy to get what I wanted.

"I keep thinking the police should have arrested somebody by now. Somebody would have seen a person out in the halls after midnight I would think. Right?" *I was failing at this bright idea.*

"You asking us?" The freckled boy said without taking his eyes off his phone or slowing his thumbs.

"Well, sure. You guys probably get around the entire resort and saw something. Like somebody out when they should've been in their room." This was still gossip, right? I don't count asking teens blatant questions, they apparently need direct talk to compete with texting.

"Mmmmm, maybe. Like the blondish guy in glasses was sus that night. He was salty from yelling with his wife." The brown-haired boy said. Of course, I needed an interpreter.

"You mean a blond man in glasses had an argument with his wife and was out of his room? Am I close?" I was filling in the parts I didn't understand from the context.

He chuckled at my evident ignorance of slang trends, "Yeeeees. Don't know the guy's name. He's here with his wife and boy. I know my folks said he knew that dead woman somehow." At least he dropped the lingo.

"Where did you see him and what time?" I clearly had blown any sense of gossiping.

"It was about...oh, maybe one-thirty or closer to two that night. I was hanging with a girl I met and forgot the time. I heard him yell a little, a door slam, then I saw him duck into the reading room." He smiled a little brighter and his eyes gave me the once-over. *Oh please!*

"Bet the police were interested in that news." I didn't want to duplicate information.

"I didn't say anything." He shook his head no and scoffed.

"So, my theory that somebody had to have seen something is right." It couldn't hurt to try and play innocent some more. "What about you, hear or see of anybody else out that night?" I asked the freckled boy.

"Naw, but those forensics people'll catch whoever. That's how its done now, not wasting time asking people." With that pointed explanation of how police work was conducted, he went back to texting on his phone.

I played a few more games, the classic Galaga and Super Mario this time, to keep up appearances before leaving. A few times I caught the brown haired boy watching me. Not in a creepy way but in a...okay...smitten way. I would look around and he would be at a game nearby with a silly little grin, goo-goo eyes, and a blush.

I had just cleared the door when the brown haired boy that resembled a teen pop singer stepped in front of me.

"Oh hey there, did you remember something?" Maybe this would break the case wide open. Hope springs eternal and all that.

He licked his lips and looked back into the game room before speaking. "I was wondering if we could talk over lunch tomorrow. I might remember something." His cheeks bloomed a rosy glow.

What was this? Surely I was past the age of boys having crushes. Heck, they didn't have crushes on me much when I was their age. Didn't he see me as ancient? As if I didn't have enough going on with the men in my life right now without some teenager crushing on me.

"I'm attending the Resort Management conference and they provide lunch." Whew, I didn't want to hurt his feelings but I didn't want to give the wrong impression either.

"Oh, that's interesting." He seemed unsure what to do with his hands and finally stuck them in his jeans pocket. "I, um, have wanted to learn more about that. Maybe you could tell me about your job over dinner."

Dinner? Of all the topics I was here to learn about, dealing with young guests with crushes isn't covered. Not even a panel discussion. I'm sure there would be plenty to cover, have a child psychologist on the panel for advice. I should request it for next year.

"I can see how this career field might interest you. But I don't think my boyfriend would like me having dinner with you." Okay, hopefully that was a soft landing for his young ego.

"Where is he, your boyfriend?" His voice got soft, barely above a whisper. "I wouldn't think a guy would let a...pretty woman...like you out of his sight." If he weren't struggling with each word it would be ridiculous. He barely got the word woman out at all.

"I'm pretty independent that way. I don't need a lot of chaperoning at my age." I cringed at that sentence. I was far too young to say *at my age*.

"Independent is the new....black. That's um, well, that's good. I like independent women." He said it without stuttering this time. I nearly choked.

Oh please somebody, rescue me.   Where was a diversion when I needed one?   Give me a woman screaming her purse had been snatched. Somebody pull a fire alarm. Anything!

"Oh, hey, look at the time. I gotta run. See you around." I was power walking away.

"My name is Justin. I'll look for you." I heard him say as I rushed out of sight.

Once I was well away from the game room and down a hall, I texted Porsche. "If you're still with Johan, ask about any evidence found." While I waited for a return text, I kicked myself for running away from a crushing teen boy. I was the adult and yet I ran like a shy girl. I blame it on being in shock when he asked me to dinner. I waited a good minute or two before Porsche replied with a short, "ok."

I was looking forward to hearing how her dinner went because I had a feeling she was ready to find a guy for more than her usual month or two. But in the meantime, I wasn't quite ready to soak in the Jacuzzi. I suspected the hot water and massaging jets would be best at the end of the day so I could stumble into bed afterward.

I looked around the hall where I had ducked and my mouth fell open. I was just a few doors down from 321, Kara Caine's room. She had blurted it out at dinner, but I couldn't have missed the criss-crossed crime scene tape on the door.

I became ultra aware of the surroundings and I felt like an isolated person in an empty hotel...with a killer. It was just me and room 321. *Gulp.* For a moment I swore the door expanded out and then contracted again as if it were breathing and the room was alive. I reached up and slapped myself, just hard enough to reign in my galloping imagination.

Surely, this was a sign. There wasn't much I could find that the police hadn't found. I understood that. I walked up to the door, fighting my fear and debating with the internal voice reminding me of the online videos showing how easy it is to still get into a room and wondered if I could manage the trick. Then the rational voice telling me that this was just some sort of morbid curiosity and I wouldn't learn a single thing.

Hey, the door looked like it was fully closed. Sometimes when you try to close these doors quietly it can rest and not latch. But surely it would be secured by the police after they processed the room. Unless somebody else saw the same videos on bypassing hotel keycard locks. There are several, but one showed using a credit card just like the old school method.

There was a deep quiet, no sounds from the game room or any other guest room. Was it possible to hear the walls breathing? In that moment, I would have believed it.

I stepped closer and pulled my sweater sleeve down to cover my hand, so I didn't contaminate a crime scene with my hand or fingerprints. I gave a gentle nudge to the door and it gave slightly, silently. I heard sounds from inside, like furniture moving. *Oh crap, oh crap. Breathing ceased.* I pulled my phone out again, dropped it on the carpet, scooped it up and texted Porsche to get Detective Larson to 321 pronto.

I turned in the direction of the lobby to wait for them. The hallway looked narrow and long stretched out, miles long, and I was all alone.

I didn't hear the door open. I knew something was wrong when I was body slammed against the opposite wall. I saw a flurry of gloves, ski jacket, and a scarf. I hit my head on the wall from the tackle and flopped to the carpet. I decided to stay down, act like I was knocked out... Don't say it, I wasn't *playing dead.*

Chapter Ten

I wasn't completely sure how long I stayed down either. Next thing, I'm being slapped, not hard but like how guys slap aftershave on, and a voice was saying, "Open your eyes, Julienne."

"Quit slapping now. I was just waiting." I managed to say.

The slapping stopped and I opened my eyes. I was propped up against the wall. *When did that happen?* Detective Larson and Porsche were crouched down around me. They helped me stand up and let go once I demonstrated I wouldn't fall over and face plant on the floor.

I pointed to the door, the police tape was ripped. "I noticed the door wasn't completely closed then I heard somebody moving in there. So, I texted you. Before I knew what happened I was tackled and the person took off."

Larson narrowed his eyes. "You didn't enter, did you?" I shook my head no and winced at the pain in my neck from the motion.

"Can you take her back to your room, I'll be up after I look around and secure the room again." He spoke to Porsche as though I weren't capable of walking.

In our room, Porsche got me some ice in towels for my head and neck. The ice had melted and I wrung out the wet towels by the time Johan knocked at the door.

He asked to use our restroom and I remembered how I had stuck the flowers in there last night.

Sure enough, as soon as he joined us he commented, "Who got that beautiful bouquet of flowers?" His eyes were on Porsche.

"They're from my kinda-sorta boyfriend." I supplied. That pretty well summed up the situation. Surprising how so few words represented a world of heartache.

"I won't ask." He dismissed it quickly since it wasn't about Porsche. Single-minded much? I suppose that comes in handy when investigating.

He took a seat at the desk while Porsche and I sat at the foot of her bed. I was feeling a little sore and no doubt I would have a bruise or two, maybe ten or so by morning.

"How's the patient?" He asked.

"I'm just fine," I said with conviction. No more of this talking about me like I was a child or not sitting right in front of them. "I have a little bump forming on my head, a sore neck, and some bruises. But, I'm fine."

There was no denying how they were acting like a couple. Must have been some amazing dinner. The room didn't look like they had taken advantage of my absence either. They were taking it slow, or the good detective really was pressed for time.

"I'll ask a doctor to come by and check on you, but that may be the morning. There was a bad multi-car pile up on the edge of town." He leaned back in the desk chair.

"Tell me what you saw. Did you see who was in the room?" He took out a small notebook from his corduroy's back pocket and Porsche handed him a guest pen.

"Not really. I saw a brief flash of a navy ski jacket and a scarf I think. I can't even tell you if it was a man or woman."

"How about height?" He made notes in his notepad.

"I was taken by surprise with the tackle and was on the floor before I knew what happened. Hugging the carpet isn't a good perspective for judging much." I spread my hands and lifted a shoulder. I felt guilty about the entire mess. I was sure my dropping the phone notified the intruder I was outside, then to be caught completely off guard and steamrolled just added to my shame.

"How did you happen to be outside that particular room?" He crossed his arms over his chest.

"I had just left the game room and I wanted to send a text to someone so I ducked into that hallway. Then I saw the tape and curiosity had me standing at the door when I noticed it wasn't really closed." I looked him in the eye because that is what happened, he didn't ask me what I was contemplating. He never needs to know of my brief flirtation with breaking and entering.

"I actually have a few things to share that I heard today." I was pleased to see his eyebrows shoot up in surprise.

I related that a teenager saw Lawsuit Chris out and about close to two in the morning that night and that he likely didn't have an alibi because the witness thought he'd had a fight with his wife. Larson took out a notebook and made a note.

"That is actually helpful. He and his wife provided alibis for each other when I talked with them. I'll be chatting with him again and see if I can shake more out of him." He had stood up.

"Were there any forensics found in Caine's room? That's the only thing I can think of to explain the intruder. He, or she, was trying to retrieve something left behind." I attempted to have the expression that children portray of complete trust they'll get what they asked for without any doubt. It's a careful cross between expectation, wonder, and a pinch of desperation. I really should be practicing these looks in the mirror. I could make a list of the most likely I'd need and run through them each morning. Without that practice, I had no idea how I looked.

He rolled his eyes and sighed. "I'm only telling you because you've been helpful with information and alerting me to the break-in of Kara Caine's room."

He crossed his arms, "There wasn't anything in the room itself, the killer likely wore gloves. There were some torn bits of green yarn and a couple of green buttons found around the body in the snow. Nothing unusual about them to help us identify anyone."

"That's all?" I asked in frustration. I'd been turning up more than their forensics apparently. Which, concerned me considerably. So much for that freckled kid and his forensics solves cases now.

Perhaps when the killer wrestled the dead weight over the balcony he or she ripped a glove, sweater, or scarf along with popping the buttons right off.

Johan ran a hand through his hair. "Our staff is on sixteen-hour shifts to cover emergencies because of the storm. That's delaying more dedicated attention to this case." He looked at his phone and strode to the door, "I have to go now and relieve another officer."

He turned once outside the door and I heard him say to Porsche, "I'll call you tomorrow." He gave her a sweet kiss and left.

"I may have hit my head, but you two seem to have had a very good date." I smiled. I moved to get the Chocolate Torte from last night's class and grabbed two plastic spoons I packed in the little dessert box. I learned quickly that I had to move slowly, the quick motions made my head swim.

We sat on her bed and ate directly from the box sitting between us.

"Come on, tell me how it went."

"Not much to tell, we had to wait for a table then he would get calls throughout dinner that he had to take." She avoided looking at me and focused on the torte.

"Gee, and somehow you two bonded and advanced to the kissing stage while he was on the phone the entire time!" *I get to push, we're best friends.* That gives me some forgiveness for pushing the privacy boundaries.

She finally looked up at me. "This is crazy, isn't it? I mean he has a job he loves here and I have a job I love in the Springs. There is no way this can work." She let out a long sigh. "There isn't a college I could get a job at here either."

Wow. Hold the phone. Was she actually considering moving here after just one date? She had never considered such concessions for anybody she had dated before.

"I don't know what to tell you. It's hard to maintain a long-distance relationship. No surprise there. But I've never seen you this smitten with any of guys you've dated to even consider moving." I shoveled another bite of Torte into my mouth. It was really good.

"That's it, what you just said. *The guys* I've dated, not men. I date guys who may be classified adults by their age, but Johan is a man." She shook her head slowly in wonder.

"Awwww. Is that signs of growth I'm detecting? And I was present to witness this milestone." I couldn't resist a little payback after the years of her hounding me to just have fun dating and not be so responsible. Ha!

"The only reason I'm not hitting you upside the head with a pillow is you've recently had a blow to the head." She stuck her tongue out.

"Look, joking aside, see how the rest of your time goes here and keep a clear head. Don't let the badge and uniform sway you, just be aware of what you really want and if that's a cop and everything that comes with a cop."

She opened her mouth, no doubt to thank me for my sage advice, but a knock on the door interrupted. I glanced at the bedside clock.

"That will be the first report from our Resort Irregulars." I jumped up and swayed just a tinsy bit. I forgot, no quick movements. I sat back down and let Porsche answer the door.

Zack darted past the door and was a bit out of breath. "Sorry, I jogged up here to avoid being seen."

"You're here now, so take a seat." Porsche waved to the desk chair the detective had vacated moments ago.

Porsche sat next to me facing Zack.

"First, I really appreciate your helping us collect anything useful toward catching the killer." I broke the ice and jumped into the meat of the matter.

"Oh yes, this is very helpful. We couldn't be everywhere around the resort. The sooner the police can arrest the killer the better." She displayed her million-watt smile. But Zack seemed immune. If anything, his eyes showed worry and his brows were creased.

"I hope we're safe. I'm staying here rather than trek to my place and back every day. My car doesn't start when it gets this cold, so several of us are sharing some rooms here."

"That's very commendable on the resort's part," Porsche said.

"It's the few rooms that they were finishing up on the remodeling. Nothing wrong with them except they're in the middle of new wallpaper or haven't replaced the old carpet yet."

"I'm surprised they're remodeling units during the busy season." I couldn't help but voice my thought.

"Those rooms were behind schedule because they had some additional work since some old plumbing needed replaced." He looked at us expecting some reaction.

"Oh, you weren't told, I guess. Well, the police found that the nail gun used to kill the Caine woman was from one of the mid-renovation rooms. It seemed best to have them occupied to dissuade pilfering any other items and doing harm." He swallowed loudly and fidgeted. Porsche and I swallowed too.

The killer was cold-blooded and calculating. He, or she, had figured out a weapon he could acquire. Seems cardkey locked rooms were no obstacle to this person, unless they were invited in. It also could indicate that the killer didn't arrive here with the plan to kill Kara, they would have brought a weapon rather than seek one out.

Zack leaned forward, "I know we were only supposed to listen for anything related to the people you identified, but something was bothering me." His eyes darted between Porsche and me.

"Well, it's just...it isn't easy to kill with a nail gun. They have safety features and well...you have to press it hard against the surface...." He turned the chair to face the desk and his hands acted out holding a gun against the desk surface. "I know I wouldn't put up with somebody holding one against my forehead. I'd fight back."

That was a gruesome little thought, but a good point. The mood flipped to dark and stifling at the idea. I suddenly wanted all the lights turned on and Johan back.

I looked at Porsche, wondering if Johan had shared anything about the case between all those phone calls at dinner. She shook her head no in response to my unspoken question. Or maybe she was just indicating she didn't have a clue about nail guns.

"I would assume Kara was um.... unconscious at that point then." I cleared my throat to hide my squeamishness. "How do you know so much about this?" I asked Zack.

"Like I said, it bothered me. So I asked one of the staff maintenance guys how you could kill with a nail gun and that's what he said." He looked back and forth between us.

"I have to say you're right. The killer somehow had her unconscious. I just wish we knew if she was knocked unconscious or if we should be listening for something else. Perhaps somebody with sleeping medication slipped her something."

"Let's keep this simple." Porsche reined me in a bit. "If the killer grabbed a weapon from a convenient stash close at hand, then he probably followed with simply hitting her unconscious. Forget sleeping meds and anything convoluted."

"I'll go along with that." I stood slowly, ready to act out the theory. "So we have a killer, carrying a nailgun to Caine's room. What next...he knocks, then pushes his way inside when she opens the door." I pretended to barge into a room. "And quickly knocks her unconscious with...the nailgun he's carrying? Proceeds to...nail her...in the head." I closed my eyes to avoid looking at them, "then to make double damn sure, the person picks her up – or drags her – and tosses her over the balcony to the frozen ground three stories below." I turned from the balcony door where my acting ended.

I turned and looked at them again to find them both staring at me.

"Yeah, probably just like that." Porsche softly said.

Silence settled like a burial cloth over us. I shook myself. "Well, does that mean our only female suspect, Debra, wouldn't be physically capable to have committed this murder?"

"Hold on just a minute..." Porsche began.

Zack interjected, "Actually, I found out Ms. Graham frequents the gym every morning and from what I heard is pretty hardcore in her workouts. She could've developed the upper body strength needed to....do all that." He stood up, nervous energy needing an outlet.

"Okay, in the morning we're going to the exercise room before my conference begins," I said to Porsche.

"Do you think you should?" She glanced at Zack, clearly not wanting to go into my recent close encounter with the killer.

"That would be why you're joining me, just in case I'm not feeling fully recovered." I noticed Zack had stopped shifting his weight from one foot to the other and was staring at us.

"I think I may have caught a cold." I wasn't going to wait and see if he bought that explanation and I wasn't sharing I got tackled either.. "Zack, did you have anything more to report between you and Kylie?"

"We haven't gotten anything on Bryce yet, but that Lochran fella that works with some newspaper. Seems he was talking to the Caine woman in the lobby and she was pretty drunk. The front desk gal said she couldn't hear but a few words 'cause they weren't yelling. Not like she did with the other realtor guy." His voice was despondent as if this was a failure.

"Do you know which she argued with first? Wade Lochran or Preston Pinder?" I wanted to be clear in my mind.

"Seems she spoke to Lochran first, then the argument with Pinder." He provided.

She was a busy woman, angering people right and left that evening. As I thought back over Kara Caine's behavior at dinner, it seemed she either thought she could smooth things over without any effort to address the issues, or she was deliberately trying to rub injuries in their faces.

"And did the front desk gal hear anything at all?"

"She said Caine said something like, 'You hypocrite, you should appreciate the public's right to know.' She said that was the only thing she could be sure about."

That was all he had to share, so we arranged to pass information during my conference tomorrow if anything else was discovered. I grabbed the empty ice bucket to have an excuse to open the door and ensure the coast was clear for him to quickly exit.

I checked on the raccoons again, showing Porsche how they had moved enough to get the blanket around themselves nice and tight. The blanket was covered in snow and I hoped that gave them some warmth like it does in igloos.

I still wanted to go sit in the Jacuzzi, but Porsche suddenly turned into a bossy nurse and asked me a battery of questions she found online. No, I wasn't confused, no *unusual* irritability, memory was fine, no trouble speaking clearly, only the slightest unsteadiness when I stood up quickly to answer the door earlier, no numbness or tingling, no loss of vision or vomiting, no headache. I just had the bump on my head that hurt when she prodded it and a sore neck.

She declared me safe to try and sleep, but absolutely no excessive heat like the jacuzzi. I groused but knew I was so fortunate to have such a good friend.

Chapter Eleven

The next day I was up early, fighting my desire to rest some more. Bruises had developed and one part of me wanted to be a kid again and take a snow day and just relax, but the information being gathered was helping in the investigation, albeit slowly in dribs and drabs.

Porsche got up with me and we both knew if we didn't just force ourselves to go the gym first thing and see Debra and her level of strength, we wouldn't go at all. I thought we might be too early and I could go back to bed, but Debra was already on an elliptical and had a sweat worked up. I fought it, but a big yawn struck and my eyes watered. I glanced to see if she saw the evidence of my desire to be in bed.

"You'll feel better once you get your muscles warmed up. I haven't seen you here in the morning before."

"I'm attending the conference so most of my day is filled and Porsche came with me as a cheerleader and motivation." I watched her face for any signs that she didn't believe me. So far, so good.

Debra was pretty average in build and height. I suppose she could have killed and shoved a body over the balcony, maybe in a rage with adrenalin pumping.

"Well, if you can stand the early hour I like how it isn't mobbed and getting time on any equipment is easier. Of course, it's probably getting more use since the weather has us trapped." She seemed to take our presence in stride. She certainly had a better attitude than last time, which made me wonder if her cheerier mood wasn't a result of Kara's death.

Trapped was a good word in this compact basement room of a snow-bound resort. I was glad I wasn't claustrophobic. The wall of mirrors along one wall didn't help the feeling either. At least the room freshener was working with a pine scent tickling my nose.

Porsche picked up the conversation, "This weather has me feeling a bit edgy. With the murder creating such tension, I sure hope the roads open soon or they lock up the killer." She got on a treadmill and began jogging.

I got on the stationary bicycle, as Porsche had advised so I could take it easy and peddled slow like a grandma. "This storm system took everybody by surprise. I'm sure most everybody here didn't expect the roads to close." Making conversation wasn't a personal strength, especially not this flipping early.

I was working on pre-caffeinated sluggish brain neurons. What if Debra was the killer? Then she would be the person who knocked me flat last night. That realization made me nervous and I no longer wanted to chat. I focused on a slow and steady cycling rhythm. But, I couldn't help but watch the suspect's every move. Would she give herself away, perhaps some sign that she had been surprised to see me this morning? So far I didn't detect anything, but then again, we were dealing with a cold-blooded killer.

Debra moved from her elliptical over to the free weights and began doing bicep curls with a large dumbbell. I counted how many repetitions she did, and was amazed when she reached thirty. She then worked on her triceps for thirty and moved to lie on a bench and did some chest flies. Yep, I was impressed, and a bit intimidated.

Another fifteen minutes more Porsche joined me. I didn't feel as stiff, but I was so done.

"Come on, you've got to get ready for the conference." We said goodbye and left.

Once we were out of the room and in an elevator, she voiced what I was thinking. "I think we can safely say she is strong and could've maneuvered a body over a balcony. Even dead weight, I think she could leverage and manage."

She was subdued this morning. Porsche had been more a morning person in High School, but maybe being caged with a killer was getting to her too.

"That's what I was thinking." Time to change the subject. "Oh, can you do me a favor today? Can you get some bread or something and put it on the balcony for the raccoons?"

"I'll get them something. I looked them up online and they can go a few days without food during the winter, but I still worry." Since they were staying huddled up, they weren't as likely to get riled. They were cute with their masks and playful look, but we both knew they could be dangerous if they feel threatened.

I had just finished showering and getting ready for day two of the conference when the doctor Johan had promised to have examine me arrived unannounced. After checking vitals, flashing the light in my eyes, prodding the bump on my head and answering the same battery of questions Porsche had drilled me with last night, he pronounced me concussion free.

"But, that doesn't mean you should overexert yourself either." He warned. I didn't tell him the gym clothes he saw out were used and he was a tad late in that warning. I was okay, already feeling tired and sore, oh I was sore. But okay.

I wasn't looking forward to sitting all day at the conference, but I dragged myself there anyway. I was in the same seat as yesterday morning with a plate loaded with a berry crepe drizzled with orange sauce, a side of cottage cheese with fruit topping for some protein, and coffee. I had a feeling I would be downing several cups of java today. Tammy joined me shortly with her own plate and coffee.

After a few minutes of nothing but devouring our breakfasts, Tammy leaned over. "I went to the Bingo last night and it proved good for gossip." She took a sip of orange juice before continuing.

"I found out that Bryce and his girlfriend had an argument later that night over Kara being here. She was really steamed, claimed he had to know she would be here and accused him of trying to make Kara jealous."

"Any idea if he was with her during the two-to-four a.m. time frame?" I crossed my fingers.

"Remember the night Kara was killed the weather hadn't gotten so bad yet, Bryce's girlfriend...I don't know her name, walked out and said she would stay in another hotel for the night." Tammy's eyes gleamed. I studied her, she was really getting into this and looking at possible suspects.

"Just remember to be very low key. Don't be obvious by asking pointed questions. Just gossip." Not that I hadn't broken that rule already with the boys in the gaming room.

"I understand. It keeps everyone safe."

"I wonder if she was back the next morning and got questioned by Johan...ummm, Detective Larson?"

"Well fiddle-faddle, I didn't think about that. I'm sure that would've been easy to have gotten the conversation around and uncover."

"When I pass that tidbit to the Detective, I'll ask him if she skipped out on being *interviewed*," I said. But, I wasn't as confident as I sounded that he would actually tell me. "But it sounds like Bryce has no alibi to cover him, so mission accomplished." I wanted to cheer her on getting a key nugget of information. She just nodded with satisfaction.

"We know that Christopher and Bryce both don't have alibis. We still need to know about Preston and Wade. Debra won't have an alibi unless she hooked up with somebody from the bar." I recapped to keep us on task.

We studied our morning workshop schedule. We would only have one workshop out of two this morning together.

We sat through the announcements for the day. It was snowing off and on now with little additional accumulation expected. Winds were gusting and drove temperatures down. The roads were still impassable as the major artery out of town was blocked by rock and snow that came crashing down the hillside in the night. Brutal cold temperatures were expected to continue.

Oh goody.

The excitement from the first day was gone. Workshop rooms looked dimly lit. Tendrils of tension and suspicion filled the rooms and our minds.

I couldn't say I wasn't affected; I just couldn't assess how much was from my close encounter last night with the likely killer, or being trapped in the resort with the killer. Plus, there was my personal specter of dealing with Mason when I got home. *Aw crud, now I was in a funk on top of sore.*

I sat through the last workshop making notes about the murder, noting all the suspects in my view and what we had so far on each. That didn't take long. Then my mind wandered to my lack lusterlove life again.

Talking with Porsche had definitely helped me identify and put into words my concerns. I had to meet with

Brandon and make sure he understood we were over romantically. I had to be strong with him, go over how we wanted completely different things in life once more, but not hurt him. Mason would be difficult since I didn't know how he handled such developments. I didn't know him very well at all. I needed to verbalize my feelings better, which this time away from the job and family was good for me in that regard.

At this point, I didn't see much future for us when he was still doing convert bodyguard work posing as the love interest to models or actresses. I just knew that left me in the shadowy wings while he was on stage for the public to see with a new woman regularly. How serious could he be about growing our relationship if he didn't see a problem with keeping me as his girlfriend so conveniently hidden?

Suddenly the workshop was ending. I copied a few notes I missed from Tammy at the end of the workshop. She took meticulous notes. We migrated to the luncheon and sat together towards the back of the room.

No buffet today, we would be served at the table so we could focus on the keynote speaker. He was the general manager of the prestigious Rosewood CordeValle in San Martin California that hosted the U.S. Women's Golf Open recently and won a prestigious travel magazine's top resort in California one year.

"Bet he misses northern California on this trip!" Tammy mused while buttering a roll.

I had my mouth full with the exquisite Caesar salad but nodded. *What a time to visit Colorado.*

After the Rosewood Corde Valle manager was finished with his talk, which I found equal parts inspiring as well as daunting.

The man across the round table blurted out, "I'm getting tired of being stuck here. I go from activity to activity in the evening, but I'm getting cabin fever. How bad could it really be out there?" The man had picked at his salad. Yep, people were becoming restless. This wasn't good.

The highly polished lady next to him jumped on his comment, "I wouldn't risk the roads, search and rescue were called out yesterday because somebody thought I-70 road closure wasn't for four-wheel-drive trucks with chains. Plus there was some landslide or something." She leveled a serious look at him.

"Four-wheel drive doesn't mean four-wheel stop." Three of us said in unison. It was the common saying in Colorado. Every winter there were people who thought they could go anywhere in any weather in a big-assed four-wheel drive truck and they usually slid all over the road and caused wrecks.

I was just out of high school one nasty winter in my little vintage VW Bug and I passed a huge fire engine slid off the road. Dad taught me to drive in snow and ice with a basic rear wheel drive car. But, I sure wasn't going to get out on those suicidal roads, even with a killer loose. But, this was an opportunity to redirect the conversation.

"The murder investigation has had delays with the weather, too." I tossed the comment out like I had yesterday and hoped somebody grabbed the ball and ran. It was a different group so it might work again.

The same restless man leapt on my comment like a wild cat on fallen prey. "If the local yahoos aren't up to the task, they should defer to Denver. They can't keep us against our will because that woman went and got herself killed. I have half a mind to call the Governor."

I pushed my salad plate away, annoyed at his barb toward Detective Larson who was run ragged. I wanted to keep my mouth shut – really I did, but it wasn't on the menu today.

"Yes, I'm sure the governor hasn't been pulled into the disasters happening around large portions of the state from this storm system and is just sitting waiting for your complaint." *Ooooops, was that me?* Guess I'm definitely getting a little short tempered as well. Everyone at the table glanced my way and I fully expected push back.

Instead, I got a wink and several smiles. Tammy had a hand over her mouth hiding her big grin.

The main entrées were placed in front of each person, I had the grilled Salmon over pasta with a white wine and basil sauce that teased the nose with soft aromas promising a sublime experience. Tammy had the Beef Bourguignon with a cognac broth that wafted over in a sultry breath.

"You would defend the local badges since your roommate is getting cozy with that one detective. Half the resort is talking about their dinner last night. Unseemly." He was downright huffing. If he had seen Porsche when she was in full out seduction mode, no telling what he would have thought. Was he stuck in the nineteen-fifties or something? Porsche may dress to impress men and turn heads, but she didn't believe in public displays of affection – or desire.

"I wish people would talk about who the killer could be instead of two people having a lovely dinner." Tammy just had to toss that into the fray. *Go Tammy!* I wanted to high-five her.

Several people from tables in the vicinity gave us annoyed looks. Would our table end up like a British soccer match and have a brawl? I looked around the table again.

The weather report lady was really on a roll. "Well, I think the 'ex' did it. I hear she made his life hell. I certainly saw her nasty side when she tore into that realtor fella." She cut her beef, "I can't imagine living with that temper directed at me and not snapping." She took a dainty bite.

Her comment seemed to be what was needed to loosen the other's tongues.

"That was over a year ago when they split, but the realtor could have snapped that night after her tirade. She really cheated him over on a deal, too. That could've hurt his reputation and business."

"Yeah, Preston looks good for it. But I think the poor guy who lost his house to a major road project she knew about could've snapped too. Did you see how she rubbed it in his face at dinner that night?"

"Oh come on, what about that editor guy? They really go at each other on the newspaper message boards. Calling each names and getting mean and ugly. She was always trying to show how he was a hypocrite. I can see how that would get out of control if they got into a fight in person." Another man at the table supplied.

"They spoke in the lobby and they weren't arguing at all. Not like with the realtor."

I had to nudge the conversation in the alibi direction. "What about during the wee hours of the morning the Detective was asking about? Surely there was something suspicious? Can't imagine a woman gets brutally murdered and nobody saw somebody up and walking about."

Sometimes it felt like taking them by the hand and leading them to the topic I needed without just asking directly.   They didn't seem to mind or even notice my course corrections.

"Oh well, that's the big question." Tammy backed me up. She was enjoying being a sidekick.

"I don't know of anybody up and around at that hour. This isn't Vegas you know."   Weather report lady said. Which was a good point. Who would be up and about at that hour?   Did the hotel staff work a midnight shift? Conversation on the murder died out and a few discussed the keynote talk.

I took a moment to look around the room full of resort management professionals and felt a sense of pride that my career aspirations were coming true. I noticed one of the big solid wood entry doors opened and the kid from last night, Justin, stood there looking around. He had an eager look on his face. I had made the mistake of telling him I was here for the conference.

I quickly slid down a little in my chair so I was hidden. I positioned my hand to block my face. I kept peeking. He began to stroll around, scanning the tables. Wasn't he a determined fellow? Finally, after a couple of minutes he left. Could my life get any more complicated?

Chapter Twelve

I had barely seen Zack and Kylie as they were hustling to get attendees served lunch with only two other servers. Considering how overwhelmed they probably were today, I didn't expect they had much new to report but I needed to find out if there were midnight staff on duty Thursday night through Friday early morning. They might have heard or seen somebody. Surely Johan would have asked already, but I wanted to check...because I'm thorough.

The rest of the lunchtime didn't produce any information from my tablemates and I half listened to their banter. The dishes had been cleared and a small dessert was being distributed.

"More coffee with your dessert ma'am?" I looked up to find Kylie.

"Yes please." She moved closer to pour and indicated with a tilt of her head toward the exit doors to hotel proper. I nodded I understood and watched as she topped off a few more cups around my table and the next until the carafe was empty. She walked to the back of the room and sat the empty coffee carafe on a table and exited through the doors.

"I'm going to go freshen up before our afternoon sessions," I said to the table in general and casually followed. I caught up to Kylie in a side hallway leading to guest rooms.

"I wasn't sure you'd have anything to share, you've been so busy."

"I won't deny that, we've been overwhelmed with this luncheon and less staff to cover than usual with the weather situation 'cause folks can't get here on the roads for shifts. I have something, just don't know if it's any help." She took a breath and I nodded to encourage her.

"Well, I heard some people talking and they're discussing how Kara was talking with some woman and they were having a whispered argument. That's how they put it, clearly upset and disagreeing with finger jabbing but in hushed voices. You know?" She was getting excited.

"Was it Debra Graham?" I dared to think this might be a break.

"That's just it. It's a Leona Dolman. She's here by herself and hasn't had any contact, as far as I can tell, with any of the other people you had me listening for. But if they argued, it may be important." She looked at me with anxious eyes and I realized it was likely even outside the resort's rules to even divulge the little she had, but she recognized it could be critical.

"You're right, this is completely new and may just help to reveal more. When was the argument?"

"Earlier in the day before Kara's brazen dinner performance you witnessed."

"Is there any way you can perhaps point this woman out to me?"

We walked over to the grand staircase that led downstairs with a view of the lobby if you stood on the landing between floors. She scanned the hubbub of people checking the activity board, going to and from the three restaurants, going to the pool or spa, milling around in the lobby, or migrating to an activity.

"I don't see her anywhere. But she tends to eat dinner at Maximilian's at 5:30 to 6:30 like clockwork. I could meet you outside tonight and point her out to you." She seemed concerned this woman was important, and I couldn't help but think she may be onto something.

"Okay, I'll be there." Then I remembered what I needed to ask her, "By the way, was there a front desk person on the night shift the night of the murder? Because that person may have seen something."

"Yes, of course there was. I don't know who that might have been, but I'll try and find out."

"It would be good to know all those who worked overnight and somehow get them to share if they saw any guests about or anything unusual."

She nodded and trotted downstairs. I returned to the luncheon just as it was disbanding and everyone scrambling for the afternoon workshops. I grabbed my things from the table and fought the throngs to get to my desired workshop. I settled into my seat at the class on privacy issues as resort management.

I sent a quick text to Porsche inquiring if she expected to see Johan today since I had some news. She replied he might make it by late afternoon or evening. The workshop was about to start so I quickly texted "Add Leona Dolman to our suspect list and find out what you can about her please."

I knew she had said she was going to attend a paint and wine event this afternoon, so that might offer some excellent gossip and information collection. I was glad she was staying busy. This isn't the vacation she expected and I felt a tad guilty about that. I had wanted to attend it as well and was terribly tempted to skip some of my conference. Reason took over and I recommitted myself to sitting through the fire hose of information from each session.

I was anxious to hear back from her so naturally time crept slower than molasses in winter. I was in my second workshop of the afternoon, a lively look at the luxury bistro hotel trend and its impact on larger hotels and resorts. I was on the precipice of either snoring or my head hitting the table when my phone gave a soft ding indicating I had a text.

Porsche was short and to the point, "Leona was in the Paint and Sip event. Johan coming by for a quick dinner." My breath caught when I read it and several people glanced my way. *Oh please, the lady unwrapping her peppermint made more noise.*

Her message only made it harder to sit through my next session on exceeding guest expectations. Rather than risk the peril of snoring, or perhaps worse drooling, I added notes in the back of my notebook on the additional information from Kylie and conversations during lunch. I tried to see if any obvious evil mastermind emerged. No such luck.

I managed to even take some notes on the session. When we were dismissed I waded through the stream of attendees again. I began to empathize with Salmon's furious fighting upstream. I saw Tammy and elbowed my way over to her side.

"I have a name to add to your list, Leona Dolman," I whispered in her ear so nobody could overhear. The press of the crowd still jostled and propelled us forward.

Tammy asked in return with a tinge of excitement, "A new development?" She was as interested in our information gathering endeavor as Porsche and I. I whispered the new tidbit about the argument and her eyes danced. Had I created a sleuthing addict?

What did that say about me? I had to face the fact that I had begun picking up the gossip the moment I heard of the murder. I was just fortunate Detective Larson chose to consider my efforts as an informant's role.

If I were asked why I could say I like to solve puzzles or some such. But in all honesty, I didn't see it as unusual to want to understand what happened and why in murder. I just couldn't ignore there were probably people around who knew pieces or parts of the full picture and just needed the opportunity outside of an interrogation to share.

I answered Tammy with the basics, "Leona had an argument with Kara, no idea what it was about. Just a good idea to keep an ear open for anything about her. I don't even know who she is yet." She nodded.

"I'll go to another activity tonight and see what I can pick up on the grapevine. Bingo was fruitful, maybe I'll do that again. Besides, I won a hundred last night." She winked at me.

I didn't bother checking the activity board but headed for my room immediately. I had my night planned. I was meeting Kylie who would point Leona out, then dining at Maximilian's for my surveillance duty. Since it is the most upscale of the on-sight restaurants I'd get an opportunity to wear my nice dress I packed. After that, I was finally going to swim and hang at the Jacuzzi like I'd been planning since we arrived.

I checked on the raccoons, still huddled there. Each time I passed the flowers and got a nose full of their perfume, I felt a twinge of some emotion. It was either regret or sadness.

I dutifully called for a reservation at five-thirty and they barely squeezed me in since I agreed to one of their smaller tables. I did request a good view of the dining room in hopes I'd be in a good position to surveil. This was my big splurge since the meal would be the most expensive part of this conference.

I spent some time actually applying a touch of makeup, put on the flowing jersey dress in a rich plum shade with black lace around the scoop neck and the black strap heels. I had to walk back and forth in the room to practice since I hardly, like never, wear high heels. I did stumble a few times.

Porsche burst into the room and stopped when she spotted me. She let out a long whistle.

"Ummm, whatcha doing?"

"I'm having dinner at Maximilian's tonight while you and your new boy toy have your time. Why?"

"You look beautiful and a girl usually dresses up this nice for a guy. One she has, or she's hoping to acquire." She put a hand on her hip.

"Don't you give me that attitude. None of your lip young lady." I shot back, but it didn't seem to faze her. "I haven't gotten to dress up and be taken out and wined and dined by Mason. Are you really going to ruin giving myself a treat?" I could give a guilt trip as good as anybody else.

"Additionally..." that's always a sign to surrender, "I don't require a guy to dress up and feel good," I said. *So there, and take that.*

She raised her hands. "Okay, uncle already." She rolled her eyes just like when we were in high school.

"So this Leona gal was in your painting class? What's she like?" I looked at her then behind her, "Hey, where's your painting?"

"I left it for them to use as an example. I didn't want to bring it home." She remained standing and talked.

"Leona Dolman is either incredibly shy or very closed and cautious. I think it is the latter. After your text, I made a point of trying to chat with her. She barely said ten words to me. I don't think it is a stuck up thing, either. She's lovely, not beautiful, and not just pretty. Poised too." She began changing out of her jeans and getting ready for her date.

"Is Johan coming up or are you meeting him? I can tell you details of the second, or I guess it's third-hand news by now, that we gathered on Leona." I figured they would like to focus on the little time they got together considering the interruptions of his duties rather than my relaying information.

"Don't think I don't see what you're doing. But I'd like to have him to myself as much as possible. Thanks." She was flipping through her dresses she had hung in the closet.

So I shared what Kylie had told me and it occurred early on the day we arrived, even before Kara's loud display over dinner and the subsequent argument with realtor Preston in the lobby. I looked at my watch, I had a few short minutes before meeting Kylie.

I handed my phone to barefoot Porsche to take my picture. "I had hoped to get a photo of us throwing snowballs or in front of the hotel, but this will have to do."

"Give me a seductive look and you can send it to Mason. Let him eat his heart out." She had a wicked smile.

"I don't know if I should. I haven't really heard much from him since the flowers. To be honest, at this point I'm not sure we're going to be together much longer so why give a false impression." Just saying it made my heart squeeze.

If she felt a little sorry for me, it'd take it. *I mean seriously.* Once we talked on the phone there was little more from him, as if the flowers and a hurried text or two just smoothed everything over and he could let me dangle. He had to have a few minutes before he fell asleep to call at the least. I was done with the short text messages.

"Suit yourself. But maybe he needs a reminder of what he left dangling here at home. A reminder you're here around some wealthy men and looking mighty good while he's in sunny California." Her eyebrows danced.

"Okay, take the picture. But no guarantees I'll send it." Which was easier said than done. Putting on a dab of makeup is one thing, walking in high heels took practice, but trying to look sexy or seductive wasn't easy for me. Porsche coached me into poses and how to look at the camera, all of which she deleted.

Finally, she told me to close my eyes and picture the best kiss I'd had from Mason. I relived the heart-pounding kiss after the first self-defense instruction he gave me. Then she whispered for me to look at the camera as if it were Mason.

"Perfect. That worked. Must've been a smoking hot kiss." She smirked. I blushed down to my toes. It had been a great kiss. If only that beginning hadn't been the closest we'd been thus far...well, no use going there.

I grabbed my phone and walked to the restaurant to meet Kylie, careful to not trip or stumble. I took the elevator because I could envision the disaster of me in high heels on the grand stairway in everyone's view. The elevator doors opened and I swiftly looked around the lobby. *Justin at two o'clock. Crap.*

I stepped out of the elevator and behind a fake plant to the side. It seemed he might have been looking around for a while already. I think he discovered when the conference dismissed for the day and had staked out the restaurants and the activity board to catch me. Resourceful. After what seemed like an hour standing in heels, but more likely was about ten minutes, he left in the direction of the game room.

I skittered across the lobby towards the restaurant, much more than a shuffle was too dangerous. I waited a few minutes before Kylie jogged up next to me. Without a word she led me to the entryway of Maximilian's, she looked around and then pointed from behind a menu to one corner.

"Okay, the dishwater blonde gal in the red sweater with a navy skirt over there. That's Leona."

"Great, I'll be dining here tonight and see if anything transpires. Porsche will tell the detective about her and I have a feeling Miss Dolman may get *interviewed* tonight before he leaves."

"I have to run, I'm assisting an activity. I'm dead on my feet and want a hard drink and relax as soon as I'm off shift.

I hope my paycheck is worth all this." With that she left, obviously walking slower than I had seen her before.

I checked in for my reservation and asked if I'd have a seat with a good view to people watch. *Yes, I used those words.* The maitre d' smirked ever so slightly.

I was led through linen covered tables adorned with candles ringed with flowers, rich polished wood walls, and glasses and silverware clinking. I was soothed by soft strains of smooth jazz. My small table was tucked along a rich wood paneled wall with a great view of most of the main seating area, and direct line-of-sight of Leona Dolman.

To my right sat Realtor Preston Pinder and his wife in the middle of their dinner. He wore a suit and tie and she was in a nice dress. They appeared bored, both scrolling or texting on their cell phones and ignoring one another. Leona seemed to pay them a passing interest.

I got serious with my menu figuring Leona was still looking at her menu as well so I had time to order, eat, and watch. The menu had sticker shock value, with some meal prices not listed. I hope I didn't yelp out loud.

I opted away from an appetizer since I wanted to be finished and ready to follow Leona whenever she left, plus it was cheaper. I hadn't planned on that course of action, but sitting here I knew I would follow her no matter what I told myself. I decided on butternut squash soup and Chilean sea bass. I was pleased to see a note that they use the greenhouse to grow most of the vegetables. I even indulged in the recommended Riesling wine to go with the sea bass.

The wine arrived with my soup and I settled in and relaxed with the subdued surrounding conversations lulling me. I let my mind wander over the puzzle that was this case. Very little evidence left behind but green yarn and a couple of green buttons. So far nobody had seen a person on her floor even during the hours of interest. But plenty of suspects who had grudges or issues with Kara Caine, realtor extraordinaire.

I was in a reverie when Wade Lochran and his wife were seated in my view. I glanced at Leona and she looked over at the couple too. She stared for a while, but just when I would have thought it was getting suspicious, she began looking at another table and took a sip of her red wine. She stroked a beautiful pendant necklace around her neck as she gazed around.

My dinner was delicious and the wine was a perfect pairing to highlight the flavors. I noticed a few glances my way and I realized Leona and I were the only solo patrons in the restaurant, and most of the tables were couples. I felt very alone suddenly. I told myself that others were here alone, like Tammy.

I determined Leona declined dessert, and therefore I did as well. She finished signing her bill and walked out when I signed for dinner to go towards my room charges. I hurried to catch up with her and noticed she took the grand stairs up to the second floor. I followed behind at a slight distance.

She had just used her key card towards the end of the guest hallway when I turned the corner. I slowly walked past and ducked into the exit stairwell with the door cracked so I could watch. I was making this up as I went, but there was no way I could stay here on stakeout in these shoes. The relaxed and contented feeling from dinner fled to be replaced with tension. What was I thinking? What would I witness standing here?

Clearly, I hadn't thought I would actually stake out a hotel room. I was surprised by it myself. It was ten minutes later when Detective Johan Larson knocked on Leona Dolman's door. Ha, I knew he was going to interrogate her tonight. I mean "interview" her. Hope he and Porsche had a nice dinner between work duty.

They were standing in the doorway as he asked her questions. Johan had just gotten to the third question when Wade Lochran and his wife returned from dinner and strolled up the hall and entered their room further down the hall from my hiding spot. They both took a slight interest, like when cars slow to drive past a wreck. I stood very still, not daring to breathe, willing myself to be invisible. Wade and his wife closed their door with a thud. I was softly shifted from side to side to relieve my sore feet. Finally, the interview was over and Johan left down the hall.

Chapter Thirteen

I slipped out of my hiding place and took my shoes off. I wiggled my toes. I didn't want to go towards the lobby to traverse over to the other wing to my room in case I should run into Johan. I went back into the exit stairwell, the cold cement felt good on my aching feet, and trudged up to the third floor, nearly ran past 321, and then all the way over to my room.

In my room, there was no sign of Porsche and I suspected she was trying to squeeze in every moment possible with Johan. I shook my head, I was worried about her this time. My phone rang. Not Mason. Aunt Regina, checking in no doubt.

I spent around ten minutes assuring her that so far we were warm and safe and I was busy with the conference. Then the conversation took a different direction.

"Dear, you know I'm not much of a computer person. Felicia was showing me that Google page thing, and well..." I swallowed and braced myself. "We looked up Mason because I didn't think he was really a gambler. Dear, where did you say he was this last week? I don't know how to tell you this..." Great, my humiliation was complete.

"Did Felicia explain that he takes bodyguard jobs?" I tried to make my voice nonchalant whether I felt it or not.

"Oh, she explained some story. I just don't understand posing as a boyfriend if he has a girlfriend already." Yeah, you and me both. She gets it.

"I'll talk to him about all that. Okay?" Since I already planned on just that.

"Is that it? That's all, you'll talk to him. I can tell you're keeping something from me. What's going on?" *I wasn't even thinking about Kara Caine, how did she do that?*

"What are you talking about? Keeping something from you? What gave you that idea?" Because I need to know what gave me away. *So not fair.*

"I have known you all your life. You're not fooling me, I can tell." That really didn't help me.

"I already told you about possibly having to stay longer with the weather and roads." Just then I had an idea. "Say, we have a guest here that apparently is one of those love her or hate her type people. You ever heard of Kara Caine?" It was a long shot at best, but maybe she knew something.

"I know she's a realtor in town, she runs ads occasionally in the paper. Hmmm, she's a bit confrontational at city council meetings and such. Kind of a flame-throwing type personality instead of reasonable, which isn't that unusual on the paper's webpage where people argue all the time. She's like an attack dog with the editorials since that Lochran fella is just like Ms. Caine, just opposite sides of any topic. He and his wife are always involved in local politics and stirring the pot with his opinions on women's place which sets the Caine lady on the warpath. She is single-minded in her tearing apart anything he says. I can't think of anything else."

I was surprised she even knew about the paper's message boards, let alone followed them with her continued proclaiming of how she doesn't get the computer thing. Besides that, I hoped I had sidetracked her. But, that also told me the police had kept Caine's murder quiet, possibly using the storm to give them time to uncover the killer for when they do release news on the slaying. That won't last long with the town's people knowing, word was bound to get around before too much longer.

"Well, I want to go get some laps in at the swimming pool. I'm ..." She interrupted me.

"Oh no you don't, tell me what's bothering you?" She had the mom voice that told me I wasn't getting out of this.

"Ummmm, well...it's Porsche. She's met a man and seems to be really smitten. She's different this time and I fear the fate of a long distance relationship." Okay, all that was true technically. Sure, I was purposely omitting significant information. Ssssssssso?

"Porsche huh? Well, I've been worried about that girl since you met her in high school. Let's just give her some space to figure this out." Whew. I hope Porsche wouldn't mind how I used her to redirect my aunt.

I wasn't about to tell my Aunt Regina there was a murder. She would have my uncle Lars waiting first in line for the roads to open to rescue me. Which is well and good if I were a teenager, but not necessary.

We finally said goodbye and I put on my swimsuit with a short terrycloth cover-up, some sandals, and an oversized bath towel. I slipped my cell phone, room key card, and some cash into my cover-up's pocket to have a drink, or two if I felt really daring. *Yeah, that's me – living on the edge!*

I had been looking forward to this and found myself wanting to skip down the hall. I didn't because sandals and skipping were an evil conspiracy meant to trip me. I knew this from experience during my clumsy teen stage. Let's just say wardrobe malfunction doesn't begin to explain the humiliating end result to a summer at the pool. It's safe to say, I'll never skip in sandals the rest of my life, at least I hadn't chipped my tooth on the lifeguard's watch.

The tall windows were beautifully frosted over with the humidity of the pool and Jacuzzi. The smell of chlorine mingled with whiffs of mixed drinks. The pool had several people playing water polo and about three-fourths of the chairs or loungers were occupied or reserved with a towel. The jacuzzi had several people but could fit me easy enough. I picked my chair to leave my towel and coverup and my feet walked me right over to the cash bar, completely of their own accord.

I decided to go with a tropical cocktail.

"Do you make a rum punch?" Not everybody served this drink.

"I certainly can, and they are gooooood." The young woman smiled.

She had fruit juices on hand for the children, so she had the key ingredients. She splashed orange juice, pineapple juice, cranberry juice, grenadine, raspberry rum and spiced rum in a glass with a couple ice cubes. I closed my eyes and took a sip, the tropical flavors and fruit juice smells conjured Tahiti in my mind, beachside on a hammock watching the waves break.

"Oh, that's a mini vacation in a glass," I whispered. Just what I needed to forget the snowy isolation.

I settled into a spot at the hot tub and said hi all around. There was a couple from Florida (oh, the Ritz-Carlton in Naples flashed in my mind) with their good friends here to ski. They seemed to take the situation in stride and joked they could actually say they had been snow bound after this. One other couple was from Texas and here primarily for their son to snowboard. Dad pointed with a thumb to the pool where the son was playing water polo.

"What brings you here? Skiing or a romantic getaway?" The lady from Florida asked me. For once in my life, I was bothered by the question. Specifically after Aunt Regina's concern over the reports of Mason with that starlet.

"No, I'm here for the Resort Management Conference." I plastered a smile I didn't feel on my face.

The man from Texas scrunched his eyebrows, "You work in resort management? Like the check-in gal?"

"No, I'm in the management training program at my resort. I'll manage resorts when I'm finished with the program." I was irked by the belittling comment, so I didn't explain that I started at the front desk before I got the trainee job.

His wife swatted his arm and gave him a glare. "Don't mind him, honey. He's a dolt." I smiled at the wife and took a sip of my drink. I know I was supposed to listen and be on duty, but the warm water and jets were loosening the bruises from last night and the visit to the gym this morning. I could feel my muscles relax. I rested my head back against the rim and closed my eyes. My bruises probably showed on my shoulder where I hit the wall and my hair was going to frizz out with the humidity, but I didn't care.

I was analyzing my reaction to the man's comment, entertaining the thought that I was realizing I would be alone when I took a resort job elsewhere. The downside to my dream career and wanderlust, I would need to deal with homesickness and loneliness when that time came. In the midst of my heavy thoughts, the conversation around me intruded.

"...what about that slighted friend? Serious anger issues with that one." One of the Florida women said.

"Remember her saying she hoped to dance on Kara's grave one day?" The lady friend replied.

"That's right, she did. I remember it clearly." One of their husbands answered.

I really wanted to tune it out, but I just couldn't convince myself to let the comments go. "When did she say that, if you don't mind my asking?"

They looked at me, startled. The woman who swatted her husband for his snide remark explained, "Well, it would've been in the bar that night when we heard about Caine's confrontations at dinner with two men. The wait staff began talking about it and once she..."

"Debra, I think her name was Debra?" One of the husbands supplied.

"Once *Debra* heard it was Kara she went on a rant. I'd never heard of the woman myself, but the place seems to have several people staying who know her." Wow, chatty lady when she gets going. They must have encountered Debra before Porsche and I met the inebriated version.

"I know she said Kara took credit for her work and won some award. I don't buy it. Had to be more there for that much anger." A husband interjected.

Good point Sunshine State man. Porsche and I felt she was strong enough to have killed Kara and shoved her over the balcony. But did she have a more compelling motive to kill Kara? Did that award have a cash prize? Or could Kara have...I don't' know...stolen her boyfriend or something? Because that is certainly rage inducing. *Cough.*

I decided it was time to do a little computer investigating when I went back to my room. I needed to see what information was out on the information superhighway on all the suspects. But, I wasn't done with my drink or relaxing.

The chatty Florida wife kept it going, "Well what about her ex? There had to be something more there than how she treated him, they divorced a while ago."

The other Florida woman finally added, "I saw Kara talking with that Bryce fella's girlfriend. She just can't let him be happy I think. She told the girl she wasn't Bryce's type, said he would dump her when somebody more suited to him came along, somebody with money. I swear, it's as if she was trying to get killed."

That was probably what spurred the argument Bryce had with his girlfriend and why she had left for another hotel. Kara Caine sure excelled at pushing people's buttons, but this time somebody snapped and shut her up for good.

The water polo match ended. I crawled out of the hot tub with reluctance and forced myself to do a couple of laps, stopping to catch my breath a few times. That was about all I could manage and gathered my items to return to my room.

I still had another day of the conference, which had been extended through the afternoon rather than end after lunch since nobody was rushing to catch a plane home or checking out. They were adding some discussion panels.

I entered my room to find Porsche was back and whistling...a love song from a movie. This was new territory. How had this happened so fast?

"You're mighty sappy with that song." Maybe I could have gone easy on her, but I didn't know how else to start the conversation.

I got my own pajama top thrown in my face for my efforts. "Don't burst my bubble toots. I'm enjoying this sensation that others have talked about and now I understand."

I stood with my mouth gaping open. How *do* you conduct an intervention? Because she was going home in a day or so, a matter of mere hours, and the love songs will turn to crying in your beer…err wine songs.

"Kylie stopped by just to say nothing new since she had talked to you earlier. I said you'd catch up to her tomorrow. But I got a little tidbit of news. Seems Bryce's girlfriend who left him in a tiff returned early the next morning to gather her items and took a cab to relocate to another hotel. All before the roads had gotten so nasty.

"That's pretty specific, how did you find that out?"

"One of the doormen was happy to talk with me." She smiled bright. I chuckled. I just bet he was.

Later, we were each in our beds and Porsche talked about her growing feelings for Johan. It was like sleepovers when we were in high school. She had it bad for Detective Larson, with no real idea of what a cop faces regularly and how a life with him would be many compromises on their time together. But I could only be there for her.

Chapter Fourteen

I was up a little early the next morning sitting in bed with my laptop. I tried a search for Kara and awards. I found her business website as a realtor with a section dedicated to her awards. An "I love me" award wall some might say, I suppose it is good for her work. *I guess.* There is a fine line between self-promotion and self-aggrandizement.

I opened a second search window and looked up Debra Graham. She was self-employed with her own grant writing business. I finally found her listed as a volunteer for a big charity luncheon from a few years back. I went back to Kara's awards page and saw the same year and charity she received an award. Maybe this was the award that Debra rants about stealing from her. Kara had several awards but Debra had none. Recognition was important.

I poked around a bit more and finally found a photo in the local paper that showed Kara at the luncheon with the executive director of the charity. Behind Kara posing with the director was Debra looking much like a deflated balloon, not envy but genuine pain.

I felt I had discovered the moment that any friendship that might have existed came to an end. The photo didn't give me the full background or details of what happened. But it was clear that Kara being buddy-buddy with the charity director in the photo had deeply wounded Debra.

In light of how Kara acted at dinner my first night, I can believe what was captured in the photo was intended to rub something in Debra's face, show her up in some way. I think the award going to Kara was the extra thrust that drove the proverbial knife deeper into her back and caused the bitterness easily brought to the surface today. But, did it make her snap? Could Kara have flaunted something recently that pushed Debra too far?

I should have stopped there, shut the laptop off and gotten ready for the conference. That would've been the sane thing to do, but I looked up Mason and got plenty on him and his *client* at a Hollywood hotspot. They were sitting very close together and he looked to be whispering in her ear. I shut down the laptop and jumped in the shower.

Even if he was keeping everything strictly business and only acting like they were a couple as his cover, it still hurt. I don't think I could ever get that picture out of my mind. I vigorously scrubbed my hair with shampoo as if I were scouring my mind of the last several days of celebrity photos out of my memory. I didn't know all the words to the Rodgers and Hammerstein Broadway hit *I'm Going to*

Wash that Man Right Out of My Hair so I hummed the tune with gusto. Humming doesn't allow for much conviction.

But it didn't change the sick-to-my-stomach feeling. The fact of the matter remained that I didn't know him that well. He swore to me he wasn't a playboy, but does a man who claims he knows what he wants (presumably me in a long-term relationship) give me limited time this early in our foundational phase, does a man continue to take jobs that require him to pose as a boyfriend if he is serious about us? I ask you.

Sure he sends flowers, an occasional text, and sporadic phone calls. But I didn't know him any better than last fall with the limited time we've had together. My feelings bubbled up, all the uncertainty with Mason, the anxiousness from being trapped with the killer, even a little bit over the death of Brandon and my failed dating, and my concern over Porsche. It all came gushing forth and I let tears roll down my face in the shower.

I had a new resolve by the time I toweled off. I had opened myself to working with a counselor on my relationship issues. It was scary and intense work. But Mason clearly wasn't ready for the long-lasting relationship he claimed he wanted. It was a... crying shame because I believe I was finally at that place. I wasn't going to delude myself that I could change him either. That was a useless pursuit and I was so done with those.

I was somber and subdued when I got my breakfast items this last day of the conference and sat in the same spot as the last few days. I normally would have loved the eggs benedict with smoked salmon covered with real hollandaise sauce, but this morning I just had some oatmeal. I wouldn't have tasted the gourmet breakfast anyway.

I got my second cup of coffee when others finally started arriving. It wasn't just me, everyone was less boisterous. I figured the fact it had started snowing again had everyone collectively holding their breath or swearing under them. I was in no hurry to rush home to Mason living smack dap across the street and Brandon hoping to resuscitate our relationship. I let my mind drift and imagined a few days at the Four Season Resort in Hualalai on the Big Island of Hawaii to sooth and warm me both.

Tammy had just sat down next to me dragging me from my daydream when Detective Larson stepped up to my table.

"I need to talk with you. Please follow me outside." He was grim and brusque. Tammy raised her eyebrows and I shrugged my shoulders in answer.

Uh oh, did he find out I had followed Leona and was there when he spoke to her? I didn't hear what they said, honest. Really, I didn't. My palms started to sweat and I was composing my defense. He walked all the way to the spa room of the *interview* fame. It was the same as the last time I visited, but the smell of Eucalyptus permeated the room and the small gas fireplace was roaring. This was looking mighty official. What had I done? More importantly, how would I explain myself.

He motioned for me to sit and then he began. "This morning housekeeping found another person killed."

My sharp intake of breath seemed so loud in the room. *Oh no, please no.* It felt like a horror movie where everyone is trapped and getting killed off one-by-one, only it was real. My mouth was open, my stomach churned with acid, and I wanted to be held by my mother more than ever. Johan's head dipped down a second before popping back up and looking me in the eye.

"You dug up the information about Leona Dolman having an argument with Kara. Who told you or where did you hear it?" His eyes were those of a pissed off Doberman's and I *knew* he could rip a person's arm off in that moment.

I had to tell him about the Resort Irregulars if Porsche hadn't already. Then I explained how Kylie passed the information to me feeling it was important.

He leaned back in his chair and sighed. He looked old this morning. Not wrinkle or worry lines, long hours without sleep, or anything like that. It was his eyes. They reflected anger but tinged with either regret or guilt. I could only imagine a ski town saw its share of violent crimes and I understood it had some Cocaine drug-related problems like many ski resorts, too. He had no doubt seen enough during his time in Vail, but this case was getting to him.

"You're telling me you were gathering information from a few employees and filtering it to me?" His smooth voice hit an incredulous note.

"I figured it couldn't hurt and any information that was worthy you'd follow up on anyway. I picked carefully, not just anyone. I made sure they knew not to ask questions, just listen and report." *Okay, I omitted Tammy, a guest, helping out.* But she had only gotten slightly involved. I shifted in my folding metal chair.

"It could've been worse I suppose. I was the one who opened that particular door and got you involved." He scrutinized me with a scowl on his face. "I don't think it's any coincidence Ms. Dolman was killed within hours of my talking with her.   It could be that Ms. Dolman knew something about Caine's murder, or she was involved in the same something that got the Caine woman killed." He fiddled with the pen and paper he used for notes.

So, Leona Dolman was the victim all right. If I had worn more comfortable shoes last night and stayed there watching like I instinctively wanted to...

"Did she tell you anything about the fight? Anything useful?" What the heck, I was in this deep, might as well ask.

"No, she claimed Ms. Caine was mad at her for cutting her off from a parking space. At least, that's what she claims. But if the person who witnessed the hushed but serious argument was correct about its intensity, it sure wasn't over a stolen parking space. I'm going to track down who saw the altercation." He began tapping the pen on the makeshift desk.

Over a parking place...but I thought all parking was done by valet here. Seems the detective wasn't buying that pathetic excuse either. What did that indicate about their heated spat? That it was personal and maybe something Leona didn't want anyone to know. Which means it could be anything.

I took a deep breath, "How was she killed? Another nail gun? Are you thinking it's the same killer?" I am not morbid or a ghoul. *I swear.* It could be important.

"The hotel locked up the nail guns that were being used in the remaining rooms undergoing renovations. No, she was strangled then left out on the balcony." He placed a hand over his eyes.

"Wow, insult to injury. Left her out in cold, so to speak. Think that indicates something?" I was thinking out loud.

"I think it makes it damn near impossible to establish time of death to a tight window. The best we can determine is it was after I spoke to her and before the maid found her." He let out a long breath.

"Was a key card used that could be traced? Or was it jimmied? Or are you thinking she knew the person? Because Kylie said she went to a few classes but didn't seem to be here with anybody." I was chattering, a sure sign I was shaken. Probably because I was watching her room only a few feet away in that stairwell. Fortunately I didn't see the killer, and hopefully the killer didn't see me. *Too close.*

"Initial evaluation of her room tells me she was surprised by the attack, so either the killer was let into the room and she trusted that person, or the killer by-passed the lock."

I remembered the online videos that had me thinking I could get into Kara's room to look around. If those videos were to be believed, it wasn't hard at all. The easily bypassed key-card system was going to be my prime lesson from the conference for Chad, I guarantee you that.

"Hey, isn't that newspaper guy and his wife on the same wing and floor as Dolman? Maybe they heard something." I hoped that knowledge didn't seem suspicious. I shifted in my chair again and leaned forward.

"Yeah, I'll be talking to them after you." He scrubbed his face with his hands in obvious frustration. "Plus the damned snow just had to start back up. We were just getting traffic and emergency issues under control."

Time for me to leave, he was stressed and I didn't want to get on his bad side.

"Did you want anything else from me?" He shook his head no.

I returned to the conference to hear the last of the weather report. Snow for today, if we're lucky it will stop by nightfall. Not much accumulation expected. Then the announcer was handed a paper.

He cleared his throat. "One final bit of news. There has been a second death. The police are calling it suspicious and will be investigating. They may need to go through the workshops and begin questioning people."

The mood went from sedate conference attentive mode to paranoid and panicky in zero to sixty. Mouths were gaping open and eyes bugging out. Then the room exploded in noise.

Who was it?

What are the police doing for our safety?

Is this a serial killer?

Dear Lord, we're stuck here with a serial killer picking us off.

And my personal favorite: Is this the Shining Hotel?

Come on, everybody knows the book's famous haunted hotel was in Estes Park, not Vail. Geesh.

It took ten minutes to convince people to move to their various sessions. I was in an event planning session with the promise to "make dealing with client's easier." I laughed internally, that'll be the day!

I sat through the session letting my phone record everything for me to review later, while most people gave up any pretext of caring. I was busy looking through my notes on what myself and the Resort Irregulars had pieced together so far. Bits and pieces mostly, scraps.

Bryce Caine, ex-husband claims an abusive relationship and I can't discount it from her behavior, and he had an argument with his girlfriend over Kara's presence and probably doesn't have an alibi. Did he snap a year after the divorce, or maybe revenge is best served cold?

Christopher Burns is suing Kara believing she knew his house would be in the path of a major road development, he has no alibi since he also had an argument with his wife and supposedly spent the night in the reading room.

Debra Graham, the slighted and betrayed former best friend had said she wanted to dance on Kara's grave, has no alibi I was aware of, would likely be strong enough to kill

Kara...but to strangle a struggling woman was another thing. She was plenty strong though.

Wade Lochran, the newspaper editor who seemed to have a running public feud with Kara on the paper's message boards for the whole world to see. He reportedly had a discussion, no raised voices, with Kara in the lobby and she said something to the effect "as a newspaper editor, surely you understand the public's right to know." As far as I knew he was in his hotel room with his wife that night.

Then there was Preston Pinder, a fellow realtor who had a heated argument with Kara in the lobby over a real estate deal gone wrong and he lost some earnest money her clients never gave back and it hypothetically hurt his reputation and cost him money. I couldn't see that as a motive, but I found it hard to even understand the passion remaining for him to have a yelling match. Perhaps Preston holds grudges and doesn't let them go, in which case Kara likely continued to prod and poke the anger like she did with others.

Of course, there was the mysterious Leona Dolman who had a hushed but heated argument early on my arrival day, before all the other suspects had their encounters. She was staying alone, so she presumably had no alibi. Not that it mattered one iota now that she was dead.

If it was difficult finding information on the handful of people who were prime suspects for one murder, then connecting a killer's motive to two deaths was double the headache. What in the blazes did Kara and Leona have in common? Kara pissed people off at every opportunity. Could Leona have angered the same explosive person? But, even with the stress of being stuck by the storm, treacherous temperatures, and icy roads out of town, nobody seemed explosive. Stressed and suffering from cabin fever, sure. Whoever the killer was, he or she seemed to be very good at hiding their murderous nature.

I thought about how many arguments there had been yet nobody can say what any of them were really about. Two murders and nobody is jumping with their hand up to say they saw somebody around those times, suspicious or otherwise. Of course, Leona's is a pretty wide time-frame. I estimate from about ten o'clock when the detective was at her door to when the maids found her, say eight-thirty-ish because Johan came to talk to me just before nine.

I was guessing the cleaning crews had a challenge with everyone stuck at the hotel (roads still weren't safe for even hotel transfers), so they probably started early because they had plenty of doubling back to clean rooms that were occupied first or even second go around. That would explain her body being found so early.

What about the green sweater thread and green buttons found in the snow with Kara? I wish I could examine them on the outside chance I might place them to a person. Although, thinking over the last three days I saw at least eight or so men and women wearing green sweaters or flannel button shirts.

But, this time the killer might have left more evidence this time. How did the two connect? Johan thinks Leona knew something about Kara's death or was involved in what got Kara killed. But what if I had been right and somebody, Leona, had actually seen a person out that night? I hadn't found if Leona had been at the pool or the lounge drinking late that night. She could have seen the killer out, perhaps a little ruffled? That was a pretty iffy motive. Maybe he or she slipped up this time. I was hoping for a fingerprint.

The session was over, not that it had been much of a learning experience. Most people were in semi-shock or couldn't stop talking. I stopped my phone recording and hoped I got the speaker and not the multiple nervous talkers around the room. Sadly, I had more questions than answers from reviewing my notes.

I texted Porsche "Are you having dinner with Johan tonight? I would like to tag along and catch up." I hated to impose on the two lovebirds, but his scant personal time was definitely going to be interrupted anyway with the second murder.

I plodded to the next session and found Tammy. I plunked down next to her.

"Everyone is ready to be done with the conference. By now people are typically energized because they'll be going home shortly. Not this time, so people are just frazzled." She looked at me with concern in her eyes. She was a kind person, sort of motherly.

"Then another death and people are getting scared and feeling trapped," I added.

"Think they'll cancel the masked party?" She asked. I noticed her face showing signs of the prolonged tension, she looked older today.

"I imagine the police will be consulted about having a few hundred people wearing masks running around at a big party. They'll make the call whether it's riskier than being in your room." I surmised.

Tammy swallowed and grew pale. I had just scared her. *Way to go LaMere.*

I ducked into the main meeting area where they were setting up for the final lunch to get myself more coffee. I was tired, but mostly I was hoping to chat quickly with Kylie or Zack. I was in luck, Zack had a trolley of items just going into the lunch area. I caught up with him and had to talk while he worked.

"I wanted to ask you or Kylie if anyone has spoken to the maids to see if they saw anybody out and about." He looked at me with vacant eyes. I noticed his movements were mechanical. He was in a bit of shock too.

"I don't know, don't think anyone was seen out for Kara's...Anyway, cops asked us already. But, nothing seems to make a difference. I'm quitting once we get the heck through this." Uh oh, I sure hope I didn't contribute to his decision.

"Zack, you know I'm attending the resort management conference. I work in management for a resort, and this is not common at all. Give it some time before you give up a good job." I tried to keep emotion from my voice and be levelheaded when I really wanted to shake him out of his funk.

"Yeah, uh hum." But his eyes were still vacant and he kept swallowing. He didn't even look my way, just kept his slow placement of items on the buffet table.

I guess everyone handles the stress of being confined with a killer who's struck twice on the loose differently. At least Zack wasn't pushing pandemonium and spreading haunted tales.

Chapter Fifteen

Before the last lunch of the conference, I took a few minutes to call my Aunt Regina and update her that the roads weren't open yet and I was safe. Okay, maybe that last part was a little white lie, but I wasn't going to have her worrying and getting my dad into the mix. I really just wanted to hear her voice. She was the closest thing to a mother I currently had and I needed her.

My call to Aunt Regina was short, which was a good thing since commotion from the lobby had gotten progressively louder and raucous.

I made my way down the grand staircase enough to take in the noise I had noticed all the way on the second floor. It didn't look good. A crowd of about thirty people had gathered, voices raised, facing the local police. Detective Larson, Johan, was between them and the front desk with five regular beat cops in uniform. I searched the crowd but thankfully Porsche wasn't present.

"You can't keep us here to be killed off. I'm checking out and you're not stopping me." A red-faced man with his luggage and coat across his arm yelled.

Johan visibly squared his shoulders, "Hear me out, folks. Maybe I can't force you to stay here..." He was channeling his inner drill sergeant.

The noise increased as everybody was attempting to be heard and the group seemed to surge forward. A stab of pure fear rose from my feet to my brain as if it were contagious and I'd contracted it. I wanted to run in a sheer panic, but I held tight to the railing and stayed rooted on the stairs observing.

Johan jumped up onto the check-in desk, "Listen to me, right now." But the crowd was getting out of control. The five patrolmen put whistles in their mouths and let loose an ear-shattering shriek until everyone, myself included, covered their ears.

When the shrill whistles ceased, quiet was restored. Everyone stared at Johan or wiggled fingers in their ears.

"You have to remain calm. If anyone leaves, I can guarantee you the killer will follow you out, perhaps even check into the same hotel you run to in your blind panic. You won't have gained any safety, but you'll have opened the doors for the killer to get away with murder." He let that sink in for a moment, or maybe he was taking several deep breaths and trying not to wet himself. Because I sure would have. I couldn't tell which, he had a great poker face.

"We have taken extra precautions, we'll now have representatives, some are patrolmen, and some are citizens we have recruited, in all the guest hallways and they will have a list of who is staying in each room. You will show your identification to this person who will ensure you are entering your room. This will start at three this afternoon so everyone has time to retrieve and carry their identification on your person."

It was at least something to keep the guests safe. Although the zealot exodus troops muttered and groused about the inconvenience, it seemed to have worked. The near-riot was averted. I took a shaky breath and tried to stop my knees from quivering. *That was close, too close.*

The crowd was finally disbanding and going in all directions. Johan glanced up and saw me on the stairs. He waved me down.

He met me at the bottom of the stairs. "You okay?" I nodded. I reminded myself that most resort managers never had to face such a mob. The chances I would deal with such a situation in my career were small, infinitesimal even. But then again, I didn't think I would see it this weekend.

"I'd like to meet with your irregulars along with Porsche and yourself by four o'clock in the Alpine meeting room. Please let everybody know. I'll talk to Porsche."

"Where is she, I thought she would be with you." My voice was squeaky like I hadn't used it in days.

"I've been too busy so far today, she is waiting for me to join her for lunch." His eyes bore into mine. "I didn't want her to see me face them down." I gulped. I could understand that and I was glad Porsche was spared the fear I experienced. I nodded.

"I'm going with you to make the announcement for the conference about needing identification to enter rooms." He escorted me up the stairs and into the conference.

Entering the conference luncheon room was like entering a different reality. The attendees had gotten their lunches and were seated listening to the speaker. All was calm and the heavy doors had kept any noise from the lobby away from this little pocket of calm. I fully understood the need to keep people busy and their minds off the situation after this stark contrast between guests with nothing to do but panic and the conference attendees who were kept occupied.

I settled into the seat Tammy had saved for me. Johan was at the podium whispering in the speaker's ear. The speaker stepped back and motioned for him to step up to the microphone. He gave the same explanation to the group, and although there was some grumbling, most people seemed to be relieved at the extra measures.

I know I sure as blazes was happy the police were able to scare up enough people to monitor the halls. That was something like twelve people to oversee the different floors and wings throughout the large square layout that surrounded a central courtyard.

I got a plate of some food and forced myself to eat. My fork shook in my hands until I calmed down fully. Tammy eyed me and her mouth flattened into a grim line.

"Can you join me to meet with the good detective at four o'clock? He wants to chat with everyone I've used to gather information."

Her eyes grew round as dollar coins, "I'll be there, dear." She swallowed then added, "What's got you shook up? Was there another....?"

"Oh no, no not that. There was an angry crowd in the lobby trying to leave. It could have easily gotten ugly but Detective Larson got it under control."

Her mouth formed an O and her eyes seemed to get even bigger. "I hadn't thought of that possibility." Yeah, neither had I.

The afternoon session wouldn't start until fifteen minutes later to allow everyone to go to their rooms and get the required identification before the deadline.

It was harder and harder for me to sit in sessions with my mind going over suspects. There must be something we were missing somewhere. Surely there is something from Leona's murder to incriminate the killer. I just couldn't seem to make any concrete connections.

I saw Kylie as I made my way to the last session of the conference. I stepped up next to her.

"Can you meet with Detective Larson at four in the Alpine room? He wants to talk to those of us helping out." I whispered.

She nodded okay and looked at her watch.

"Let Zack know please."

"Sure, and I got your message about the maids. Guess we should see what Larson says first."

"Yeah, I guess." I was non-committal. I was hoping he didn't sideline the Resort Irregulars. We had to pull out the stops to get the killer.

For the first time I began to wonder if the killer would get away with these murders. Once the roads opened, the mad rush to vacate the hotel would begin.

Forensics and the fine details took longer than on TV and small towns probably had to send some things to a larger and better equipped city forensics lab for testing, likely Denver in this case. Not that there was much from Kara's room, but even if evidence was left at Leona's murder, the testing may be too late and everyone scattered.

The session was going around me and it seemed participants were giving the workshop their attention. Except moi. Of course, who knew what was really taking place behind those attentive looks on the exterior? This was one of the added on sessions to make up for being stuck here and it was twice as long as the usual. It droned on, and on.

My mind drifted to Leona. Why kill her? She had argued with Kara and was even a suspect to a degree. Did Kara and Leona have something in common? Perhaps they both knew something worth killing over. Or could they both be involved in something illegal? I was going over the same scenarios and I only came up with more questions than answers.

The session finally ended and we made our way to the large room where we congregate in the mornings and for lunch. There were some final announcements and then handouts for everyone on next year's event which would be held at Allegretto Vineyard Resort in Paso Robles California, plus an evaluation of the conference. They reminded us to only judge the conference and not include the events in the resort that were out of their control. I was keeping a copy of next year's handout. I never heard of this resort, but I would love to see a vineyard resort operation.

The conference had kept me sane during this cloistered experience. I sure couldn't handle the whole cloistered nun life – not that I ever considered it because of the whole celibate thing. I was a bit unsure how I would handle full days without the conference to occupy my mind. How had Porsche been handling her days other than the painting and wine activity? Good question. She didn't mention taking part in many activities.

I had a half hour before meeting with Johan so I ran down to the activity board to see what was happening tonight that might interest me. Mask making was happening for the gathering tomorrow night. Apparently, the kids hadn't made enough for everyone. There was a pool shooting competition and another cooking class. Bingo and other reliable standard offerings.

Oh…they were having a Vegas themed night with poker and craps table tonight. Winners would get credit in the gift shop. I suspected that they did these gambling nights often enough to have the equipment on sight. That might be a good diversion and perhaps still hear some gossip. It was also another good leisure interest to note for my home resort.

I was reluctant to meet with Johan but dragged myself to the Alpine conference room anyway. The room still had some glasses on the tables from the conference attendees. He was standing and Porsche sat, quiet and reserved watching him. I sat next to her and we hugged.

Kylie, Zack, and Tammy joined us and I nodded to Johan. I guess Porsche never got around to recruiting any irregulars, she was too preoccupied. Only half lighting was on, so it was softer on the eyes. I could practically smell the anxiety in the air. I briefly introduced Tammy and how we met. I included the gossip she had provided from Bingo night as a reminder.

"Thank you all for joining me. The death of Leona Dolman has been determined officially as a homicide. I don't think that comes as a surprise, most folks already assumed it. The problem I have is two-fold." He raked a hand through his short sandy hair as he stood with feet shoulder-width apart.

"We don't have much evidence. The crime scenes aren't yielding anything that will be useful in the next day or two. Once the roads open and folks scatter to the four winds the chances of an arrest diminish significantly." He began to pace.

"My problem is in using civilians, all of you. We have gotten more immediate leads through your reporting of gossip." He stopped pacing and stared at us, "However, it puts all of you at greater risk if the killer figures out what you're doing. This person has killed twice now and will likely be feeling the walls closing in on him with the monitors in each guest hallway."

Kylie raised her hand and Johan nodded for her to speak. We all looked at her. "I just wanted to be clear. You're wondering whether we should continue, right? "

Our heads all turned to Johan for his answer.

"It isn't that simple..." He began but Tammy interrupted him.

"But it is that simple. We want to help. We know we aren't trained like yourself. We know we have to appear like anybody else flapping our lips with gossip and not stand out, or as the invisible staff who're just doing their jobs." She looked around at each of us then back at Johan.

"At this point, it might seem even more suspicious to overtly avoid those situations. But we'll be quietly and carefully listening and partaking in gossip like the others and funneling what we learn to you. I think your dilemma is how much you need us." Tammy raised her eyebrows in either challenge to deny it or waiting for him acknowledge how much she was on the nose.

I never fully appreciated the expression *pregnant pause* until that moment where we waited in such anticipation for what Johan would say that I swear none of us breathed for a full minute or more. His face didn't give any hint at the thoughts that no doubt were flying through his mind. Finally, he spoke.

"The fact of the matter is I do need your help to resolve this as soon as possible with the time constraints bearing down on me. But I can't stress enough how dangerous this has turned out to be. I contend we have a desperate person on our hands to have risked a second murder under these close quarters." He scowled at each of us. Gee, make up your mind.

"I had a thought earlier in the day to question the maids to see who of our suspects was alone in their rooms both nights." I offered up. Not brilliant by any stretch, but it was something at least. I was running out of ideas how to uncover anything new.

"I'll get with the manager and question them again. Last time I spoke with them I was looking for anything suspicious or someone near the renovation room where the nail gun was acquired. This time I have specific names to ask about." His eyes bore into mine. I swallowed. *What? What did I do now?*

"I keep thinking somebody had to have seen something." I shook my head. "Oh...what about around Leona's room, did anybody hear anything at all?" I didn't want to mention, again, that I knew Wade was a few doors down.

"Wade and his wife are not far on her floor. I interviewed both of them first thing. Apparently, the noise of hotel rooms interrupts their sleep so they both took sleeping pills and claim they didn't hear anything. I spoke to two others on the floor as well and nothing. They didn't even hear knocking on a door in the night."

I squirmed in my chair. The idea of a ghost wasn't too much of a stretch at this point. How could two murders happen without anybody seeing or hearing anything?   It isn't natural.

Okay, I dismissed the idea of a murderous ghost who could walk through walls as soon as it popped up in my head. A ghost wouldn't leave sweater yarn and buttons. A ghost might be the one being that Kara hadn't gone out of her way to alienate.

"I don't suppose there were any fingerprints by chance?" My voice was barely above a whisper.

"Her room was wiped clean, not even Leona's prints were found."   Well crap, that would've been too easy. *Wouldn't want that.*

Chapter Sixteen

The Resort Irregulars were still operational and we left the meeting with Johan feeling resolute in searching out gossip without calling attention to ourselves. Kylie and Zack still had extra shifts to cover, Tammy was going to divide her time between Bingo and the bar. Porsche was joining me for the Vegas night and we would meet up with Tammy later in the bar.

But first, we had enough time for dinner. We still had to eat in the midst of all this, even without much of an appetite. I hadn't eaten much today as it was. We waited and finally got into the Ranchhand. I was getting tired of eating out and actually was looking forward to some home cooking when I got home. Aunt Regina's chicken, bacon, and spinach crepes sounded great about now. I settled for the chicken potpie instead and a glass of their Riesling that I had tried last night. Hard to believe that was just last night. Porsche had filet mignon. As soon as we gave our orders, I tackled the elephant in the room.

"What's wrong? I don't think I've ever seen you so quiet?" I couldn't keep the concern from my voice.

"Nothing. Nothing's wrong." She didn't make eye contact but looked around the restaurant. The whistling and bubbly Porsche had left for parts unknown and I was sitting with subdued Porsche.

"Liar face. You forget I know, I can tell. Remember, best friend over here. You know I'll just bug the crap out of you like you do me. Might as well tell everything now."

She finally looked at me and I could see sadness in her eyes. "It's finally hitting me how much I've grown to care for Johan and how I'll be leaving when the roads open." Her eyes filled with unshed tears. I hurt for my friend, but I didn't know how to help. They were good for each other, but the distance and timing were huge obstacles.

"I can't believe I join you and get snowed in with a killer and fall for a cop. All I wanted was some wicked fun with a ski instructor or something." She attempted a smile, it made her look even sadder.

"Let's have a really nice dinner with no talk of guys at all. They are a forbidden topic while we eat. You're having some wine or a cocktail with dinner and relax." I was adamant that for a short while she get her mind off the first guy I knew of in her adult life that she had opened her heart to yet the timing was all wrong.

We added O'batzten, which is a Camembert cheese with cream cheese and beer seasoned with onions and paprika spread over bread for an appetizer to our order so we could really take our time. It arrived quickly along with my wine and her rum and coke made with the German River's Rum.

"How about you treat yourself after dinner and go to the spa? I can hit up the Vegas night. With less competition maybe I'll have a chance to win."

"Actually, we haven't spent much friend time together, how about we go to the spa together in the morning. We can set an appointment now." That sounded perfect, I needed a break from the murders too.

I had my purse since it was easier to have my identification together with my phone. I called right from our table since they had extended hours through the "snow-in" and set a spa appointment for mid-morning so we could have a late breakfast. I was sleeping in since I didn't have the conference to attend anymore.

I pulled up the spa menu on my phone and we discussed what treatments we wanted. Choices, plenty of choices: standard massage with a mani-pedi, aromatherapy with your massage, deep tissue or sports massage, detoxifying mud wrap, hot stone massage, or special herbal poultice massages. We were tending towards a hot stone massage and the seasonal body wrap. I knew it hadn't fixed her emotional pain, but she was getting her mind off Johan for a little bit. In the morning we would both get a little break and relaxation at the spa as well.

We showed a slight bit of restraint by skipping dessert, but we lingered over coffee and discussed our jobs and the personalities and politics involved at both.

Porsche sighed, "Wish this dinner didn't have to end."

"I know, we have the illusion of normalcy while we sit here. You don't have to be a Resort Irregular, you can just enjoy the rest of the time here. It's okay, I understand." I wanted to offer her an option, an out from being involved.

"No, I am the smart sidekick. You need me."

"I thought it was *plucky sidekick*?" I grinned. "But I always need my best friend."

"So, Vegas night – should we dress up a bit or save that for the masked ball tomorrow night?"

"Let's stop in the gift shop before it closes and see if they carry any resort fashions."

I had only glanced in the gift shop when we arrived. We were greeted immediately upon entering. There were the standard supplies of items guests might need but didn't pack. There were branded items and men got a rack to themselves of more sweatshirts and ski items. But the ladies got two racks of women's resort fashions. Sure there were more sweaters and sweater sets, but some had more bling and glitz.

We both selected an outfit for tonight, going for glam. I chose a flowing lightweight knit royal purple top and pant set with a double row of rhinestones around the neck, the bottom hem of the shirt, and around the wrists. Porsche chose a sleeveless black sheath sweater dress with chunkier stones around the neckline and a belt with matching stones.

At the checkout, I noticed a display next to the register of sleeping aids.

"Have sales gone up for the sleeping aides through this ordeal?" Just making conversation, really. I had the silly idea sleeping pills would account for nobody hearing either murder if they were zonked out.

"No, only sold one box. The couple couldn't agree on whether she needed them or not. He sure thought she did. That was three days ago and none have sold since."

"You'd think more people would need them, considering everything." Of course, guests might have brought some from home. I finished and paid for my new fashion items. I would never forget this trip, but this fashion choice would remind me of the fun Porsche and I managed to have in spite of the murder.

We changed and freshened our hair then made our way to the makeshift casino that was two of the large conference rooms combined.

Before us lie the room without all the long tables from the conference, but rather seven poker tables, two blackjack tables, a roulette wheel, and a craps table under softer lighting. Sounds of subdued conversation, shuffling cards, tossed dice on green felt, and a rolling ball on the roulette wheel greeted us. I was surprised at the amount of equipment they owned. At least I guessed they owned it all since the roads weren't good enough in town for even rental companies making deliveries. Besides, last I heard most of the businesses were still closed.

We picked up our free chips, if we lost all of those we had to purchase more. I knew next to nothing about gambling. Since 1991, Colorado had a few mountain towns like Cripple Creek and Blackhawk with legal gambling. But I had never visited, let alone gone to Vegas.

"I'm going to need to study how this works for a while and get the hang of it. Don't let me hold you back." I told Porsche.

"Okay, I'm going to play roulette." She left and I had to deal with how all of this reminded me of Mason. From his Sheltie named roulette to his playing in high stakes poker tournaments. You can see why he seemed like every guy's fantasy. My heart ached at the thought.

I thrust Mason from my mind, again. Which in itself was sad. I had this handsome and exciting guy in my life and more and more I had to put him out of my thoughts because he caused me such disillusion and second thoughts about being with him. I pasted a smile on my face and determined to go forth and conquer.

I wondered around the modest crowd and watched a Texas Hold'em Poker game. It wasn't anything like the poker that my dad taught me to play during family game nights. There were handouts of how to play and I grabbed one.

It starts with only two cards dealt face-down and that told me it was different than the poker I knew. These two cards are called my "hole cards." Based on just those two cards you bet, check, or fold. At this point you are betting on "the flop," three shared cards that will be dealt face-up in the center after the betting. Betting again for a fourth shared card face-up coming called "the turn", then a final round of bets on the fifth shared card face-up called "the river". Then the betting for the pot of chips begins for real.

After the flop was dealt, or initial three shared cards are dealt, you bet on the strength of what your two cards plus the shared would make for a hand. You can only count five cards, so the directions advised to bet the best five-card combination of standard poker hands − like three of a kind − from your two face-down cards and the shared cards in the middle. The best combination hand wins the chips.

I watched for several hands. I understood there was likely more of a strategy to playing this kind of poker, but I wasn't picking it up that easily.

Debra was playing at the table I watched. She was oblivious to my presence and seemed a competent player, winning about as often as not.

I strolled around and watched the craps table which had lawsuit Christopher and his wife playing. That was a game that seemed to be the epitome of gambling, and thus not for me.

I turned and bumped into Justin, standing looking around. *Crap.* No way to avoid him when I run right into him. He looked at me, his eyes looking over the new glam outfit from the gift shop and my hair spruced up a little. He licked his lips a few times and swallowed, he finally managed to get out the words, "Wow, you look...wow." I was completely covered, although I guess the touch of glitz and the slightly clingy drapes of cloth produced a subtle allure.

"Are your parents here with you?" Because I didn't think he should be here without them, even if there wasn't actual money at stake.

I barely got the words out when a man placed his hand on Justin's shoulder. "Come on son, we're at the craps table."

"Dad, this is Julienne…" He seemed unable to finish.

He nodded, "Nice to meet you."

They left and Justin looked back at me with his shy little smile on his smitten face.

I kept my ears open, hoping to catch some gossip where I could listen in but everybody's attention was on the games.

I focused on the blackjack table and players. I wasn't the only one, I stood with several others looking at a little handout on how to play and observing a few people at a table. It stated the object of the game was to beat the dealer. If you go over twenty-one points you lose. The object is to get more points than the dealer without exceeding twenty-one. Then the instruction sheet listed all the values such as the ace (one or eleven points), and all face cards are ten points. A "blackjack" combination of one ace and one face card was the ultimate and beat all other combinations.

The dealer deals two cards out and takes two cards for himself with one showing. Then he starts to the player on his left and goes around. The instruction pamphlet gave five options at this point: stand (no more cards), hit (take a card), double (taking one card and no more that hand), split (which confused me about splitting your hand into two hands – sounded like cheating to me), and surrender (which I feared would be my typical.)

"My first time with Black Jack. You?" The man standing to my left asked. He was around my age and dressed in slacks and a lightweight black sweater. I glanced around for his girlfriend, but he didn't seem to have a lady with him at the moment.

"Total novice here. I'm glad they provide instructions." I handed him mine.

"I will break the stereotype and take these directions gladly." He smiled an easy infectious grin.

I looked around again.

"Did you come here to ski, snowboard, or snowshoe?" I was pretty sure he hadn't been in the conference.

"Snowboarding with my buddies. They're over there." He indicated the craps table with his mixed drink. "What a trip this has been too. Unbelievable."

"Yes, it's been like something in a movie. You never think it'll happen to you. Stuck in a hotel with a killer." I hoped I wasn't being too melodramatic, but this was my way to get the conversation on the two deaths.

"This was a great idea to help us all relax." He was close, in my personal space. "Can I get you a drink? Wine perhaps." His smile seemed genuine and if things weren't up in the air with Mason I might have spent some time talking with him.

"I don't want to give the wrong impression. I have a boyfriend." I smiled to soften the rejection.

"Oh. Where is he?" He didn't look around but stayed focused on me.

"He's on a business trip." I shouldn't feel like I had to justify his absence, but I did.

"*Business* trip. Well, his job must be important to take him away from you." He cocked his head.

I didn't know what to say, so I didn't answer. I turned my attention back to the table. Before long he moved to another table. I let out my breath.

"He lost interest fast. You're better off without getting close to a guy you don't know, considering the murders and all." It was the lady to my right with a slight Boston accent. She looked to be a few years older than me, but not many. She wore glasses and was dressed in black slacks and a red sweater for a classic look.

I smiled, "That's very true. I'm Julienne, and you are?"

"Lisa and this is my friend Blair." Blair was noticeably taller than Lisa or myself with a fireplug shape dressed in a royal blue velvet blazer, gray shell, and black slacks. We shook hands and took a step back from the Blackjack table to talk without disturbing the players.

"I was here for a conference. I guess your skiing got canceled." I had to start somewhere. It was rude to dive right into the murders.

They were indeed here for the skiing and as a winter holiday. They both lived on the east coast and had to work through most of the holidays so this was their break.

"It's a shame your belated holiday break got waylaid with the tragic events." Witness my clumsy attempt at introducing the murders. I hoped I wasn't rushing the conversation.

"We've kept busy, considering everything. I loved the baking class but tonight looks to be more fun." Blair supplied in a stronger Boston accent that made me smile as I tried to decipher what she said.

"I wonder when the police will make an arrest. There are enough people here who had issues with her. Maybe even enough to kill Ms. Caine. I haven't heard anything about the other woman." I couldn't give a bigger invitation to gossip without flashing neon lights.

"Oh, Leona was a sweet woman. She was in our baking class and we hit it off. We had drinks after class and enjoyed our dessert creations in the bar." Lisa contributed.

"I don't think I've spoken to anybody who'd gotten to know her. I was beginning to think she was a mystery woman. I mean, she wasn't here with anybody. Just seemed so... shadowy or secretive." I let my voice get carried away like I was a teenager again.

Blair's hard Bostonian voice shared, "Not at all. She was meeting up with her love. I guess the storm must've hit before he made it. This would be a romantic getaway."

"She seemed sad he didn't make it, so we didn't talk about it much," Lisa added.

How interesting was that? Did Kara argue with her over this man? Could Leona have taken the man from Kara? That would have infuriated a woman like Kara and could explain the intense argument they had. There were so many possibilities and no way to narrow the focus of speculation.

"Yeah, she had a lovely pendant necklace from him that she kept holding. You could tell she missed him. Rather sweet really." Blair tossed out.

"What did the necklace look like?" I wondered if it was the same necklace she wore at dinner the other night.

"It was a white gold heart with several rubies. Looked expensive." Blair said.

That was the same necklace she wore at dinner when I observed her...okaaay, when I was on stakeout and followed her. I didn't know if it was important, but if it was expensive, maybe the killer kept the trinket. Could it have been a robbery gone wrong? I'd tell Johan. He would know if she was wearing the expensive token of love. Maybe the killer slipped up finally.

Two of the players at the table were leaving so Lisa and Blair saw their chance to play. I wondered to another table that was also changing players. I was still relaxed from dinner and didn't feel much pressure to win, only to enjoy the game.

I was cautious in my play, but I was a fast study and won a few hands. Before long I had amassed a substantial pile of chips. Between hands, I looked around and saw a modest crowd around my table. Porsche was watching with a genuine smile and her phone out...taking a picture of me I think. Since this wasn't really Vegas she wouldn't get in trouble.

For the next several hands I did well, not great. I decided Porsche had waited on me long enough so I played the last round a bit more aggressive to be done for the night. I had a ten and queen for a score of twenty. I stood with what I had and didn't take any more cards.

The time to reveal our hands came and the dealer had a six, a two, and a king for eighteen. I won a pretty big bet this time.   My heart was pounding and I had the biggest smile on my face. I don't think I had ever won anything before and this took a little thought and some luck.   Of course, I wasn't playing in Vegas against more experienced players.

I got the chips added to my stacks that had slowly grown. I was surprised at how many there were now. I gathered them up to get my gift store credit and joined Porsche.

"That was great Julie. I streamed it live on Facebook and tagged Mason. He needs to know how good you are at Black Jack."   She shook her head side to side like a bobblehead, proud of her virtual prodding of Mason to pay attention to me.

"Oh, I don't know.   Maybe you shouldn't have done that."   I wasn't going to try and make him jealous or anything like that.

"Too late now, honey. Let's cash that pile in. I'll help."

"Did you win anything?" I asked, hoping she had good luck too.

"Of course I did. We'll have fun picking out more from the gift shop."

I wish Mason had been here – I would've liked to share my beginner's luck when with him. *Sigh*.

Chapter Seventeen

I was shocked when they added up my chips and it came to six hundred and fifty in chips, and that was after subtracting the initial chips they gave me. But that translated to sixty-five dollar credit at the gift shop. Wow, what would I get? I hadn't looked at their jewelry in the display cases, maybe I could get a nice gold choker chain. Or better yet, souvenirs for Aunt Regina, Uncle Lars, and my cousins Felicia and Loring.

Once we had walked out of the Alpine-room-turned-Vegas, I shared with Porsche what my new acquaintances Lisa and Blair had told me about Leona.

"I wonder if Johan knows he will need to contact her boyfriend and give him the bad news?" Porsche said.

"I wonder if he found any contact information for the guy?" I thought aloud. Johan hadn't mentioned finding her phone. But then he probably wouldn't share if he had.

I checked my watch. We decided it was close enough to our meeting time to go ahead and get seats in the bar. The lounge was subdued compared to the other night with muted conversations and more drinking than revelry or camaraderie. After my time in the Vegas-themed room, I felt downright bubbly compared to my fellow guests seated around me. Tammy, looking sophisticated in a long skirt and sweater, walked in barely a minute after us. We were clustered around a small square table and waited for the prior guest's glasses to be removed.

Tammy let out a whistle and complemented Porsche and I on how lovely we looked.

I was tired of the snow and had enjoyed the mental break of swimming in the pool and relaxing in the Jacuzzi last night, and gambling tonight. The Vegas night was a success and I'd felt like I was in a casino rather than snowbound in a small mountain town, in a building filled with a few hundred people and a killer or two. So I wanted to continue that feeling.

When I asked for a Mojito, one of my favorite drinks, our waitress asked if I wanted regular or slushy. Whoever thought to take a Mojito and blend it into a snow-cone-like drink was a genius. I went for the slushy, with the image of warm sunshine and palm trees in my mind. This little adventure had me wanting a tropical vacation badly.

We also got a plate of appetizers. Each table had a little acrylic stand with the entertainment schedule. Sadly the local musicians still couldn't make it for performances. No telling how rural they might be and reports said the roads were still treacherous. To compensate, they had Karaoke. Fortunately, we were away from that area so we could talk, and bonus - the noise might keep our conversation from being overheard.

I was surprised I was getting the entire evening with Porsche, but no doubt Johan was stretched even thinner since the second murder. I could tell she was forcing herself to join in but I also knew she was still struggling with the situation with Johan and the approaching goodbyes. Occasionally, I would catch her staring into space and looking sad.

Once our drinks and appetizer arrived, we were ready to talk.

Tammy jumped in first, "Bingo was buzzing tonight. Seems the realtor guy, Preston, is really hurting and he blames Kara."

"I still don't understand what the big deal was about." I voiced my doubt.

"Oh, well deals fall through for one reason or another all the time. But Kara's people wanted their earnest money back when they backed out of buying the house. They changed their mind or something." Tammy was talking with her hands now, providing a flourish here and there.

"Anyway, Preston was upset because they hadn't put down what he considered the standard amount and felt Kara had purposely manipulated for a lower earnest amount. He felt she owed him more money in the first place. But Kara argues that he owes her clients their money refunded," she finished.

"That doesn't seem enough to kill a person over though," Porsche said and I nodded in agreement.

"Well, Kara took to Facebook and Twitter complaining. She supposedly never openly said his name, but it hurt his business anyway. At least, that is what he's claiming. His clientele and general business dropped considerably and his wife isn't happy to be on a budget. So his marriage is even having troubles."

"He claims it's all Kara's fault?" I was a bit surprised.

"Oh yes, she would even taunt him about the decline in his clientele. From what the ladies at Bingo were saying, she took every opportunity to either discredit him shrewdly or twist the knife to make him regret challenging her." She took a big swig of her Hefeweizen German beer.

"If the adage is true that anybody is capable of murder if pushed far and hard enough, then everything you mentioned could've been a shove over the edge. Whatever caused that heated argument may have been the last straw after a long build-up, then he's angry and takes a few hours to acquire the nail gun and confront her." I finished and shook my head.

Why would anyone purposely taunt and push somebody to such a boiling point? But it happens all the time. She had witnessed Kara at dinner the first night taunting lawsuit Chris and her ex-husband horribly.

"I spoke to two ladies who actually spent some time with Leona. She was here to meet with her boyfriend – since he isn't around they theorized he didn't make it before the storm closed the roads. Seems she wore a heart necklace with rubies that the boyfriend gave her."

Tammy's eyebrows crinkled, "How sad. The next thing the man will hear is that she's gone." Seems Tammy was tender-hearted, I swear she was slightly teary-eyed.

"We have plenty of motives to kill Kara, but why Leona?" Porsche asked.

"That's what I was wondering. Could they have something in common against the killer? If it were Preston, could Leona be Kara's client...or something like that? Something that put both of them on the killer's angry side." I was spitballing.

"You're always wondering why somebody didn't see something. What if Leona saw something incriminating for the killer and had to be eliminated?" Porsche offered.

Oh, that made perfect sense.

"That's possible, too." I sighed, "I just wish Leona had chatted up more people. It was as if she didn't want to draw any attention."

"Oh, I don't know. Maybe she felt lonely without her boyfriend, or being out with all the couples around made her feel lonelier. I can't imagine being here for pleasure without somebody to enjoy the location with, even if it's a friend." Tammy offered.

She made a good point. Even with Porsche, I was lonely. There were couples surrounding me continually reminding me I was alone in a romantic resort.

"Okay, maybe it isn't suspicious that she wasn't more outgoing. So, we think she either saw something or was associated with Kara and the killer somehow. I have another wild theory." I took another sip of my slushy, which was like summer in a glass – with alcohol. The karaoke was in full swing, currently featuring a silver-haired man crooning a Dean Martin song, so there was little chance of our being overheard. "What if Leona is with Kara's former boyfriend? I was trying to think what they might argue about and that was what came to mind."

"You mean Leona stole the boyfriend making Kara rabid mad? Porsche asked.

"I know, it's a weak theory. It would explain their argument but it doesn't explain why Leona was killed." I admitted. I grabbed a cheddar broccoli bite, dipped it in the sauce and popped it in my mouth. Yum.

There was silence for a few moments as I chewed and took another sip.

"Nope, I can't think of how the boyfriend theory could result in Leona being killed," Tammy said and Porsche agreed.

"We really need to know more about Leona," I stated the obvious.

Tammy rummaged in her purse and pulled out her tablet with a flourish. "I think there should be plenty of battery left to do some internet searches."

Porsche and I pulled our chairs over to each side of her so we could all see the screen.

She pulled up a search engine on her browser and typed in Leona Dolman. Her fingers hovered over the keys, "What city should I add?"

"Well, she knew Kara so I think it's a safe bet she has connections in Colorado Springs too," I said.

The results were broad, but after a few false starts we found a newsletter mention with a picture of the same Leona Dolman we sought. It was an announcement of her being the bank's new Private Relationship Advisor, which was a fancy way of saying she catered to the wealthy clients of the bank. The jobs were also called wealth management advisors and they dealt with financial planning and all the investing and range of products or services the bank provided, only with the personal touch so they needn't stand in lines with the riff-raff and such.

"She must've gotten paid well," Tammy speculated.

"Could she work for the same bank Kara used?" Porsche asked.

"Don't know how we would find that out," I said.

"She dealt with money and financial planning, anything come to mind with that?" Porsche asked.

We sat thinking, sipping, and munching for a few minutes. "Nope, can't see a connection. We really need more information all around." Tammy huffed.

"Check her Facebook and LinkedIn," I suggested. It had worked well for me last fall. We each whipped out our cell phones.

That was a bust too. She had her Facebook with the highest security restrictions. Her LinkedIn contained basic information only, no resume. She used it to get more clients with the bank and her financial planning role.

"Financial Planner...could she have lost somebody money and Kara...made the same person's life hell? Like Bryce." Tammy suggested. Ah yes, the poor abused ex-husband.

"I know Kara got their nice house in the divorce," Porsche said. I stared at her. "I've been listening, just not picking up any big news." Porsche smiled.

"That scenario could apply to Chris Burns too. He lost his house to a development, spends the money to get a lawyer, and then what if investments Leona advised lost money? That could break a person." I said.

"I suppose even Debra could fit that too." Porsche added. "She doesn't seem to work, so what if Leona lost her money?"

"Okay, we found an angle that might explain Leona's murder. Which isn't connected to Kara at all, but more of a two-birds-in-one-reckoning weekend scenario." I summed up.

"I'd be interested in hearing this angle you have discovered." Johan stood in front of our table, shoulders slumped and his eyes drooped.

He grabbed the last chair and joined us. I was surprised he didn't give a little kiss to Porsche like they had been doing.

"We were just tossing around why Leona might have been killed, which has bothered each of us." I shared. He motioned with his hand to keep on talking.

Between the three of us, we shared our theories of both being on the killer's angry side or saw something incriminating for the killer and had to be eliminated. We saved the financial–planner–gone–wrong aspect and the murder's convenient timing to take her out while the three of them were in one place.

"That is certainly some fine conjecture. Top notch even. But, that's all it is." He leaned back in his chair as if his back couldn't hold up much longer. I bet he was running on caffeine and sheer willpower. The Nordic handsome detective I'd met a few days ago was replaced with a haggard looking man who seemed to age 10 years before my eyes.

"I've wanted to ask you if you found Leona's phone and her boyfriend's contact information to notify him," I asked.

He sat forward, "What boyfriend would that be?" His tired eyes grew bigger and his brows crinkled together.

"A couple of women at the Vegas Blackjack tables took a cooking class with Leona and then had drinks. Leona told them she was here to meet with her boyfriend. Said her heart pendant necklace with rubies was from him." I saw his eyes flicker with interest.

"First, we found her cell phone all right. The sim card had been removed. Secondly, there wasn't any necklace with rubies, heart-shaped or otherwise." He rubbed his blond five o'clock shadow. "I'll need a description from them."

I grabbed a clean napkin and Johan's pen to draw a rough sketch of the necklace I saw her wear at dinner. I handed it to him, "Here, I saw her wear it at dinner in Maximilian's the night before I heard she was killed. It may not be exact because I noticed it from across the room." I also gave him what I knew of Lisa and Blair for him to follow up.

"Look, I've gotta go. I have to cover one of the halls for the next few hours until another person is brought in by snowmobile." He glanced at Porsche and gave her a sad smile tinged with regret. It appeared they both realized the short time they had together, but who would have suspected they would grow close so quickly? I certainly didn't see that coming. So, they stepped back from their whirlwind romance before it got too serious. Porsche's eyes showed it was too late, she'd already grown incredibly fond of the detective. Johan wished us all good night and rushed out.

Timing. I could relate. Relationships – sheesh. The lyrics to a rock ballad came to my mind "love is just a lie made to make you blue. Love hurts." Guess I still had things to work out.

"Any other ideas connecting Kara and Leona ladies?" I asked.

"To my mind, they both could have been involved in something illegal to warrant murder," Tammy said as she shook her head. It was hard to imagine what would be a strong enough reason to push a person to kill twice.

"What if these murders aren't actually related?" Porsche suggested. We thought for a few moments on that.

"It does seem like too much of a coincidence, but I suppose somebody could've thought it would make getting away with killing Leona easier since the police were already stretched thin and concerned with Kara's murder. It could've muddied the waters enough to be an opportunity the person took." I commented.

"Of course, it could be a serial killer pushed over the edge being snowbound." Porsche tossed in, seemingly as an afterthought.

"Ummmm, I don't think so. The sim card wouldn't be removed from her cell phone if she didn't know the person, like in the case of a serial killer." I said.

"So the missing sim card suggests there was something on the phone the killer didn't want anyone to see." Tammy clarified.

"Yes, like a photo, a text message, even her email or social media linked to her phone. Anything in there could be incriminating. You can even record audio. No telling what she had that the killer didn't want the police to find." I added.

"It'll take longer for the police to track down her mobile carrier and then request the records. Television shows make it look so instantaneous Johan says." Porsche enlightened us.

"The police can get the text messages and phone log information, but the rest likely went with the sim card or they'll have to find her home computer to search. That'll take time to get cooperation and coordination with another city's police force I imagine." Porsche was just full of information.

"Didn't know you were such a techie there." I kidded her. She had never seemed interested past Facebook and using her cell phone for calls and the camera.

"You don't work with college students without picking up on some of the technology." She answered back.

Chapter Eighteen

Kylie and Zack walked up and quickly sat down. "Mind if we join you? We can't very well come to your room anymore with the hall monitors in place." Kylie rushed to say.

"We can't be seen with you for long either, management is strict on *fraternizing* with the guests." Zack's voice held an edge that betrayed there was more to his comment.

I raised an eyebrow at his surprising attitude.

"Don't mind him, he's upset that the latest love of his life is forbidden to him. She's here with her parents and Zack thinks he's in love." She shared with cold efficiency and a hint he did this regularly. She rolled her eyes to top off her statement.

Porsche, Tammy, and I exchanged looks in an attempt to not laugh at the young man. However, Zack was oblivious to our hidden smiles and coughs. I almost shared how sweet it was, but stopped myself before embarrassing him.

I cleared my throat to be serious, "Anything new to report?"

Kylie glanced around then leaned forward. "I actually have a message for you. Seems Kara's ex would like to speak to the guests who have made friends with the investigating detective. He'd especially like to talk to the gal dating Detective Larson." The skeptical look on her face was like my father's when I'd told him a whopper lie. It was the "You expect me to believe that load of crap?" look.

"Well, that's new." Tammy said.

"Did he give you an idea why he wants to meet with us?" I asked.

"Something about wanting to convince you of his innocence. But I suspect he wants you to influence the detective for him." She sat back and crossed her arms and pursed her lips. Kylie might have a young face, but right now she seemed older, a touch worldly-wise, even jaded.

"Did he have a place and time in mind?" I asked.

"You aren't seriously thinking of meeting with him?" Porsche snapped and her eyes squinted.

"No, I thought both of us would go. Strength in numbers and all that. Tammy and these two could wait for us nearby." I explained in my gentle and coaxing voice – because that always worked.

"Tonight at ten in the children's craft room. But even with the three of us outside, I don't know if you should."

I looked at Porsche. She read my mind, like when we were in school, "You'll just go anyway if I don't. Okay, we'll go together. Don't make me regret this."

My gentle and coaxing voice worked again, it's better than a Jedi mind trick. Kylie and Zack left with promises to be outside the room in a few minutes waiting for us and left. We only had a few minutes before the meet.

"Wish I knew martial arts," Tammy stated.

"She's been getting private lessons from her dreamy boyfriend." Porsche blurted out, then stopped and covered her mouth.

"It's self-defense lessons and I got all of four lessons." Wanting to move away from the sensitive topic.

"I didn't know you had a boyfriend. This is such a romantic resort..." I tuned it out. For the umpteenth time, yes, it's a romantic hotel and would've been wonderful to curl up with Mason next to a fire in the Lobby watching the snowfall. I took a deep breath and ignored the squeeze of my heart and tightening around my lungs.

We paid and left to meet Bryce, Kara's ex and the most likely suspect incidentally. I had my purse with me and I now carried pepper spray with me regularly after Mason convinced me to last fall. I also had those four self-defense lessons from Mason. It was something at least, but I had no delusions it was a perfect plan.

We met outside the door to the children's craft room, which appeared to be unlocked. Then I noticed a sign on the door to pick out your mask for the party tomorrow night. For a moment I thought he jimmied the lock to the kids' craft room like the killer might have done to surprise and kill the two victims. But it seems the room was left open for convenience to pick up masks.

"Keep the door open a little, don't let it latch, so you can hear us," I told Tammy as we opened the door and entered the dimly lit room

All along one wall were seemingly hundreds of half-masks hanging, clearly made by the children. Some more elaborate masks seemed made by teens with active imaginations and talent. There were elaborate feathered and rhinestone ones, harlequin styled, then cat or dog themed, several wild-animal styled. I felt like a wall of masked people was watching.

In the half-light, Bryce was clearly sitting at a worktable waiting. He slumped, elbow on the table, and his head in a hand, which looked as if it kept his head from falling off. His eyes had dark circles and his pale face glowed in the muted light making him look ghoulish.

"Could we turn on more lights?" Porsche, the horror movie addict, asked right away. I second that request. *Gulp.*

Bryce simply pointed to the wall at the front of the room, but I looked around and saw the companion switch near the doorway we entered through and snapped it on. The bank of fluorescent overheads blinked a few times then splashed its garish blue-tinged light over the room. You would think the harsh brightness would make the masks look less eerie, but you'd be wrong. The bright light cast the hollow eyes of the masks in stark shadow making them more ominous, as if dark eyes followed me.

I looked around, we seemed alone with Bryce. My eyes searched him for signs of a weapon or an inkling of violent intent. I shook my head and drove scenes from the "Shining" that began playing out of my head

He raised his arms, "I'm alone and unarmed. I'm quite sure the two of you could take me no problem." I wouldn't bet on that personally. That sounded too close to "Trust Me!"

He lowered his arms. "I just wanted to talk, maybe you could put in a good word for me with that detective you're dating." He directed his comments to Porsche, presumably because she was dating Johan. *He was behind the times, that was so yesterday.*

"Why not talk to Larson yourself?" I didn't feel comfortable with his staring at Porsche in that creepy glassy gaze.

His eyes flitted to me, "I have talked to him. Seems just because I was married to that...woman, I'm the prime suspect. The divorce was finalized a year ago and I'd gotten on with my life. Who knew she could ruin my life even in now."

From the look of him, he was either worried about his being a suspect, Tara haunting him, or his guilt was eating away at him. He could still be the killer. But I couldn't think why he would kill Leona. Standing here the financial planner gone wrong didn't ring true and I had this nagging the two deaths were related.

There was a part of me that could relate to being the suspect for what appeared a circumstantial reason. I experienced it first hand when the networking meeting I coordinated at Colorado Springs Resort resulted in a prominent attendee murdered. I still couldn't shake my doubts about him though, or maybe it was nerves.

"I'm sure if you have somebody who can vouch for you that night, you know...an alibi...then the detective will look at others." Oh, I couldn't help it. Here he was asking us to believe him blindly.

"Well, that's a bit tricky." He swallowed. "My girlfriend and I had a little disagreement and she stayed the night elsewhere. She came back early and packed. She may have made it out of town before the storm made the roads impassable."

"So, you've no alibi. Did Kara's behavior at dinner tick you off?" Porsche hit him with both barrels.

I shot her an *"are you out of your mind because he could be out of his?"* look. She leveled a *"don't give me any sass when this was your idea"* look back at me.

"I didn't want anything to do with her. I wanted to leave when I saw she was staying here, but then the argument with my girlfriend happened. I stayed in hopes she would come back and we could just move to any other hotel together. Then she packed and left me, by the time I packed and was at the desk to check out and go home, they said the roads were closed. I just lost my fight after that."

I noticed he didn't really answer Porsche. I was itching to ask my own question but had my doubts about how he might react. Porsche had already blazed that trail with her question.

"What about Leona? Did you know her or maybe were a client?" I held my breath.

"I don't even know who that woman was, I could've sat next to her and not known it because I never met her."

"Look, I can appreciate the position you're in, more than you know. But, I don't know what we can do for you. The police, even the detective, won't listen to our opinions. They have to follow the evidence."

"But, I didn't do anything." He whined. It was his whine that irritated me.

"You have no alibi, you have a motive of revenge or snapping from the final straw over dinner, and you had opportunity staying here by yourself." I left out anything about the nail gun being swiped from a room under renovation. Perhaps he would mention it himself.

Porsche shot me the "*are you out of your mind?*" look after my bleak summation of his situation. Sure I was poking the bear, but at this point he seemed to be more whipped than dangerous. Of course, I reminded myself, looks could be deceiving.

"All I can do is ask you to please just...just maybe...ask the detective to....I don't know...look harder at the other suspects." His eyes pleaded with both of us.

It occurred to me that Johan must have questioned him again, and put some pressure on him, for him to resort to this last-ditch effort for mercy.   Maybe Johan was looking at him as the top suspect.

"We'll let the detective know you asked us to speak to him on your behalf. We can't promise how he'll take the news."

I turned to leave but Porsche walked over to the wall to pick a mask. "Do you really want those in our room staring at us?"

"I'll hide them in a drawer." She grabbed two with feathers and rhinestones and we left Bryce still sitting at the table, his head in his hands.

Once outside the room, I couldn't shake the creepy feeling. I did a little jig stomping my feet and shaking my arms.

"What's wrong? Did he do something?" Kylie asked with concern in her voice.

"Trying to shake off the eerie feeling from all those masks in the room watching." Now it was their turn to hide their laughing at me.

I turned to Porsche, "Should we find Johan and let him know of our meeting?"

"I'll find him and let him know." Porsche declared. I was happy to give her some time to talk to him by herself. I suspected they had more to say to one another.

We said our good nights to the others and would see them in the morning at breakfast before our spa appointment.

I was on my own and wanted to change and go to the Jacuzzi again to relax. My mind was churning over the suspects, all the motives or lack of solid motives for Leona, and all the speculation.

I was halfway down the hallway to my room when I stopped. I looked behind me and before me again.

Where was the hall monitor? Seriously, where was the monitor to check identification and keep us all safe? I felt the hall lengthen and the walls close in around me. *Maybe it's just a bathroom break.* I tried to breathe but I felt panic like a finger of ice run up my spine.

The soft green carpet seemed a sickly shade now and the hall lights were dimmer than I remembered.

Could that meeting have been to waste our time, keep us out of our room? I mentally kicked my own butt because that wasn't logical. Bryce couldn't know both Porsche and I would come to talk... unless getting one of us alone was the plan.

Another kick in the patoot, nobody can predict where a guest would be with all the activities planned. Besides, such distraction would require more than one person involved and I wasn't ready to increase the killer count.

I had almost got my breathing under control when a disembodied stage whisper reached me. "Curiosity killed the cat, Missy. You've been asking too many questions." It was a ragged whisper and although I thought it was a man, it could easily be a woman affecting coarseness to disguise the voice. I thought it came from down the hall toward the exit stairwell. I seemed rooted to the spot as if my feet were nailed down.

A door opened just behind me and to the right sending my heart into triple time rhythm. I jumped and looked back to see a man leaving his room, stop and stare at me with his eyebrows meeting his hairline.

"Where...." My voice was anemic. I swallowed and started again. "Where's the hall monitor?" If the man moved toward me, I swear I might scream. My nerves were sizzling. It was that wall of masks, they made me into a frightened little bunny. Of course, the disembodied, ominous, and creepy voice didn't help either.

"Don't know, he was here about ten minutes ago. Bet he had to take a whiz." He chuckled as he turned and walked away from me. I was torn, did I turn and watch him walk away or face toward my door?

Another door opened down past my room and I about jumped to the ceiling. The woman walked past, scooting around me.

Suddenly my feet were scurrying to my door, the key card already in my shaky hand. I watched the red light on my hotel room lock, it seemed eons before it turned green and I fumbled with the handle.

I darted inside and switched on the entry light and stood with my back against the closed door examining the room. I was shaky. I liked the solid door to my back, maybe because a killer had grabbed me from behind last fall.

I bent over and took deep breaths. *Congratulations LaMere, you scared the crap out of yourself.* I was beginning to doubt I'd actually heard a voice, I could have easily imagined the whole spooky incident. No wonder there was nearly a riot after Leona was found, guests were scared, jumpy, on edge if my reaction was any indication.

Still standing with my back to the door, I realized it had bothered me that a key suspect singled out Porsche and myself. I couldn't help that people noticed Johan and Porsche were dating and I wouldn't think that would make her a target, but I counted on the killer being unaware how interested in the gossip I had been. This trip I was getting my master's degree in gossip.

Perhaps subconsciously I was anxious that my interest had been noticed and my imagination created the voice just now.

I pushed off the door. I wasn't sure about going to the Jacuzzi now. I didn't think I could walk down the hallway again. I could fully understand why some people were afraid to leave their houses. What was that again, agoraphobia? Hell, I was quickly convincing myself that barricading myself in the room until we could leave was the best plan I'd ever heard.

I turned on the television to get my mind off the missing hall monitor and the dubious creepy whisper. Movie choices were the Texas Chainsaw Massacre, the Man in the Iron Mask, The Shining, and the Horror of Dracula. Oh goody. *Was the universe telling me something?*

At least nobody had suggested the killer was a vampire that could mesmerize Kara and Leona. A killer ghost, but no vampire…that I had heard. Although, that would explain why there was no blood around Kara's body in the snow.

Stop it! Johan had already said lack of blood wasn't unusual with a nail gun injury wound.

I palm-slapped my forehead. My imagination was running scared too. I kept flipping channels to the shopping networks and found...nail guns for a great low price. *Seriously?* I finally found a sit-com and let that play in the background. I ached for my clarinet, but I didn't think neighboring guests would appreciate a solo concert so I had left it home. At times like this, I liked to play a technically challenging piece to get my mind off of any problems. Something like the "Flight of the Bumblebee" could keep me busy for hours.

I availed myself of the mini-bar and made a chamomile tea spiked with rum. Not my finest mixology but I was working with what I had on hand. I drank my spiked tea in a hot bath with Epsom salts the hotel provided for those guests who were skiers.

I was replenishing my hot bath water, my hands and feet wrinkled, when Porsche returned. At least I hoped she was the person who entered.

"Porsche, that you?" I called out.

A knock on the door, "Can I come in?"

I pulled the shower curtain two-thirds closed for a little privacy. "Sure."

"Just checking on you, saw the mini-bar was raided." She knew I hated paying the high prices for in-room refreshments.

"Was there a hall monitor out there?" I asked.

"Yeah, I forgot all about it until he asked for my identification."

I relayed my scaring myself to near hysteria and then the movie selections, although I didn't mention the voice I heard. At this point, I was seriously questioning that I had heard anything at all. We both were laughing by the time I was done. We laughed until we cried, emotional release from the tense days I guess.

She wiped her eyes and left me to finish my bath. I toweled off and joined her. When my feet touched the floor, I marveled at the heated marble. I was getting spoiled.

She had started a fire in the fireplace and had put upbeat music on the radio. I had upgraded to this junior suite just to have the gas log fireplace. It took up a corner, was rounded and of smooth white stucco. Two chairs and a side table sat in front of the fireplace creating a little seating area.

"Did Johan share anything about the investigation?" I suspected he was more likely to share with her than anybody else.

"He wanted me to tell you no heart necklace with rubies was found in Leona's room. He didn't say anything further." She relayed the information without emotion.

"Did he say if it appears to be a robbery gone wrong?" Which I suppose was a possibility; depending on if Leona could have gone down to the bar sometime after Johan had questioned her at her door. Then perhaps came back and interrupted a resort burglar. Valuables have been stolen from hotel rooms before. But, robberies in hotel rooms typically occurred when the room was unoccupied. If the intention was to steal valuables from her room, wouldn't they have broken in during the day when it was most likely she would be gone?

"No, he didn't say. But that isn't what happened with Kara Caine. Stealing a nail gun is a bit premeditated to kill a person and certainly not from an interrupted burglary." She pointed out.

"I agree. We briefly revisited if Leona's death had been unrelated and somebody used the opportunity thinking we would lump the deaths together. What if Leona's death was truly unrelated to Kara's and Leona simply interrupted a burglar?" I explained.

"Sure, it would fit. It's logical, but I think it's improbable. People haven't been in their rooms much with all the activities to keep guests engaged and occupied. We know Leona took the baking and painting class, so she was involved and not sitting in her room during the day. I would think a smart burglar would have slipped in during the day, around lunchtime perhaps, when the risk of getting caught is lowest." Porsche conjectured. It was as though she were reading my mind.

I got up to make us some decaf coffee. "Good point, the timing is all off. Even a second-rate burglar would pick the best time to avoid getting caught in the act." I held up the coffee pot and she nodded. Once the coffee was brewing, I continued.

"Okay, scrap the burglar idea. Did he say anything else?"

"Not on the case."

"Did you talk with Johan more about your growing feelings for each other."? It sounded silly to put it that way, but it was accurate.

She swallowed.   "I ummm...we talked for a brief moment or two. Not much more to say. Long distance relationships are notorious failures. We won't have a strong enough foundation built in just a few days. So it's best to stop it now before we got too...attached." She was attempting to appear resolved with the decision, but I could tell her heart ached.

I handed her a disposable mug with decaf coffee the way she liked it. She tucked her legs under her and held the cup with both hands and stared into the fire.

"Sorry. Should I put on some crying in your beer songs from the laptop? We can really wallow. I can rant about what a pathetic man he is to let you get away. I will fulfill my best friend role fully." I was serious, but I hoped she didn't need the full treatment.

"I really want to take a pillow and hit you with it right now. No, I don't want to wallow. This whole time with Johan was supposed to be for fun, and before I knew it I was thinking of rearranging my life and moving up here to be with him." She shook her head in wonder.

"I keep hearing how finding somebody happens when you least expect it. In this case, I think the universe is being a tad sadistic." I proclaimed.

We sat in front of the fire and talked into the night about everything in our lives. By the time we tumbled into our respective beds, it was late, but we felt stronger and knew we would have each other's back no matter what came in the next days and months.

Chapter Nineteen

The next morning the alarm woke me, in a fog I slapped at it until it stopped. I dragged my feet out from under the cozy sheets and plunked them to the carpet. I verified I hadn't destroyed the alarm clock like I'd intended a moment ago. Nope, it would live to rudely awaken again.

I started the in-room coffee maker, the best alarm clock for Porsche, and showered. In spite of the late night, we made it down to breakfast on time. Since we were getting our spa treatments shortly, we opted for the quick continental breakfast spread rather than placing individual orders in the restaurant. Tammy joined us but we didn't have anything new to share.

I wasn't going to share my hallway scare. The memory of which was already waiting and the more I thought about it the more I was convinced it was my overactive imagination.

"I wonder if the killer saw the perfect opportunity and will get away with these murders?" Tammy said while artistically spreading a knife full of cream cheese on her bagel slices. It was like she was painting a masterpiece with thick brush strokes.

"I keep hoping that somebody may have seen something or know something that will be the key, the smoking nail-gun so to speak." I was struggling with some doubts, so I returned to the old premise. I took a bite of my éclair with Bavarian cream filling. *Oh. My. Heavens. That was divine.* I closed my eyes and savored.

"I can't believe there was so little evidence," Porsche added, stirring her granola and yogurt parfait.

"Well, it's a matter of time as well. Some of what the police may have collected they likely couldn't get to a bigger lab for testing because the roads are closed. It's the time frame before everyone scatters to the four winds that's killing us." I shared. They winced at my words. "Sorry, terrible choice of words."

"Yeah, I guess this was the perfect storm for a murder," Tammy added with a straight face before taking a bite of cream cheese slathered bagel.

We groaned at the storm reference.

"All we can do is keep our ears open and encourage gossip like little Nosy-Nellie zealots in hopes something will surface."

I had gotten some scrambled eggs and bacon to offset the éclair, my accommodation to nutrition. I began picking at the eggs.

Between bites of her bagel, Tammy share, "I'm going to one of those painting and wine sessions. I can't draw a stick figure, so I'm hoping the libations will loosen some tongues."

"Don't forget Leona. Maybe figuring out more clues on her life will give us why she was killed and then help nail...I mean catch this killer." I took a bite of bacon and crunched away.

"Is it just me, or is everybody about to explode from the tension," Tammy asked then folded her napkin and placed it back on the table. I was thinking about the near riot in the lobby the other day, and no doubt my imagining of an ominous voice proved everyone was on edge.

Porsche and I glanced at each other remembering my moment of fear in the hallway over nothing.

"No, I think everything has combined to create a pressure cooker of anxiety." Porsche didn't mention my lunacy last night. She winked at me. *Our little secret.*

"The weather has cleared and we may get temperatures as high as fifteen today. That may help with the roads." Tammy said.

I worried if the roads started to clear and the killer hadn't been arrested, the guests would likely stampede in Exodus out the door losing potential evidence and lessening the chances of an arrest.

I saw Kylie and Zack in the full-service breakfast restaurant and waved, but they were so busy they didn't notice me.

Porsche and I went up the lobby grand stairway and took a few moments to look out the floor-to-ceiling windows overlooking the front entry. It still looked like a solid sheet of ice on the roads. The evergreen boughs were sagging low from heavy wet snow. The bare limbs of aspens were coated with thick prickly ice crystals.

"Doesn't look any better to me," Porsche said.

I agreed.

The spa was ready for us and I was taken into the room Detective Larson had used for his questioning of guests. Guess he got booted out for paying customers. No doubt the spa was doing a brisk business with such a captive audience. Porsche got her own room.

I was going with the hot stone massage and the seasonal body wrap, so I would be here for a while. My Massage Therapist was Kandi and we chatted a little about the treatment. I lay on my stomach and the massage began. The room filled with gentle acoustic music and the smell of mint and eucalyptus essential oils while the fireplace warmed the room. I was amazed at just how tense I had been. My muscles were like bands of steel in my shoulders. *Youch!*

After a while, Kandi began placing the heated stones down my spine to help loosen muscles. Ohhhhhh, that felt good. In spite of how relaxed I was becoming, I found myself asking another "invisible" staff member about the two murder victims.

"I imagine most everyone staying here has gotten a treatment in the last few days?" I tried to make it sound conversational not forced.

"Sure seems like it." Ah, a woman of few words. Dang it.

"I keep wondering who that Leona was? She didn't seem like a ski enthusiast to be here. Did you meet her?" I know I violated the rule to not ask direct questions, but I didn't have all day to wrangle information. I tried to sound like I wanted to gossip and not like I was asking questions or interrogating.

"Uh ha."

"I hear she was by herself. That seems strange to me. Did she seem like she was here for something illegal?" I was doing the best I could to get Kandi to share.

"She didn't seem the type. Pleasant enough and knew what she wanted. Gave me a good tip." Bingo, Kandi gave Leona a treatment

"If I didn't ski and I wanted to go to a resort, I would go somewhere warm. Just saying." I wiggled the bait again.

She finally spoke. "Oh, there's a reason to go someplace you most likely won't meet anybody you know and appear to be alone. Just saying." Her massage never wavered as she dropped that gem.

She was an experienced masseuse, strong hands and arms to really work on those stubborn knots in my muscles.

"Oh, like maybe she was seeing somebody...?" I wanted her to spit it out.

"You didn't hear it from me...she was upset that her, let's say special friend, showed up with his wife in tow. She said this was some sort of anniversary for them and he ends up bringing his wife. Like a slap in the face, she said. Then she said how he could take his family priorities and shove it." She indicated for me to roll over.

"Oh my," I said. "I wonder who that might have been?" So she wasn't waiting for a boyfriend that couldn't get here because the roads closed, she was here for a continuing affair. And an anniversary of some sort, so it was a long-running affair. Well, that was quite the bombshell. Could this married man have anything to do with Kara's death too? I kept looking for a connection between the two murders.

Then I thought of a jealous wife getting rid of the mistress. The wife could've insisted on going with the husband with the intention of putting a permanent end to her husband's cheating ways. Although, personally I wouldn't strike out at the mistress – I would go after my unfaithful hobby. *Just saying.*

The entire hotel was full of couples, most of them married. The philanderer or his wife could've taken the murder of Kara as an opportunity to get rid of a difficult mistress and have Kara's murderer be the likely suspect. But, I couldn't see how the philanderer or wife could be tied to Kara's murder.

Maybe my panicking when there was no hall monitor wasn't so extreme after all if there are two killers lose.

"She didn't share anything about him. No name. No hints." Kandi added as if anticipating my next question.

"What did the police say?"

"I haven't told a soul…except you just now." Whoa, people really do confide in me.

I think Johan will want to hear this bit of information. After my treatment was finished, of course. No need to spoil my spa treatment.

Next was the exfoliating full body scrub then I was wrapped in a layer of moisturizing body mask and warm wraps. Kandi set the timer and exited. The soft music played and I tried to keep my mind active, but the long night and total relaxation allowed me to doze.

Kandi knocked on the door and entered after what seemed like only a few minutes, but had probably been twenty minutes. I tried to grasp the threads of my dreams. I remembered it seemed important, something about the killer. The dream had slipped away when I snapped awake. She began peeling off the wraps.

"With these deaths, I keep thinking about how sad it is, both the women were single. Did Kara get a spa treatment?" It would be so much easier if I could just come out and ask questions.

"Yeah, she did. I wasn't her therapist though." She stopped and crossed her arms. "Come to think of it, her attendant said she was excited about getting even or exposing something. The attendant said it sounded like Kara was a vindictive type and was just happy to be finished with giving her massage." She began removing the mudpack with a wet cloth.

Getting even may have got her killed if the recipient found out. That was good but it still didn't point out the killer. It could still be any one of the people I considered my suspects.

"I don't suppose she gave a name? I'm just concerned about being held here much longer with the weather and roads still undrivable."

"Yeah, that's rough alright. The other massage therapist said she didn't tell who she was getting even with or anything."

I met Porsche in the circular lounge around the fire outside the spa. I was glad to sit and enjoy the relaxed glow I was still feeling. The treatment had been a bit pricey, but it was so worth every dollar. Porsche had struck up a conversation with a couple and after she introduced me I just listened.

"I don't know who she was, and I spent my days in classes or some activity. Did you run across her at all?" Porsche was working the Leona trail.

"We met her, briefly mind you. She kept to herself in a reserved way, but would chat when you made the effort." The apparent husband answered. In his late forties, tanned, graying temples, and a ram-rod straight back. If I had to guess, I would say he was prior military maybe turned government contractor. I saw plenty around the Colorado Springs Resort – my home base resort.

"Where did you meet her? I met two ladies who took a baking class with her." I hadn't seen Porsche in action before but she was good. Subtle in her approach and slipped in her questions with an example. She was getting her degree in gossip as well.

The wife answered. She was equally tanned, quite fit, with mostly white hair and a gentle smile. Her perfume – White Shoulders I believe – wrapped around me, smothering me. They were the type you would see on the cover of an active retirement magazine.

"Let's see, we went to a ski and snowboard talk given by the resort ski instructor. Not that either of us is taking up the sport, but our youngest son is interested. I remember she said she'd never done any winter sports before. The instructor was giving her the sales pitch for lessons once the weather cleared a bit."

That corroborated what somebody else had told me about Leona not being here for the winter sports. But was she really here for an affair with a married man, or could a boyfriend be waylaid like we theorized?

As I'd heard over and over again, this would be a romantic getaway. But you don't go to Vail in the winter if you don't enjoy winter sports. I couldn't see the attraction of shopping in town as a big draw either, particularly by herself. So an affair was likely, or maybe the potential boyfriend was into skiing or snowboarding. That was possible – if he existed.

Sure, there was always the chance that she loved winter and wanted to be alone and enjoy the food and shopping by herself. I suppose that is possible. But the necklace that disappeared, supposedly given by a special male friend, seemed to point to a rendezvous with a man – whether a boyfriend or a torrid affair.

The lady added, "I believe the ski instructor might have been flirting with her, but she seemed uninterested."

Could be he wasn't her type or more confirmation she was seeing somebody.

"Do you think these horrible deaths could be connected? I don't want to be alarmist, but two killers is a terrible thought." Porsche appeared to really play up her role and gave a shudder.

"It seems highly improbable to have two murders in our small numbers without them being related." The stiff husband answered.

"I heard she argued with that brash uncouth woman who went over her balcony." The wife tsked-tsked. "But I can't imagine how they would know each other, can you James?"

"I don't know, but at the poker table last night one of the men thought this Leona knew another guest, he thought the man suing Kara was talking to her in the bar in a...very cozy way – if you get my meaning. He couldn't be sure, but that's who he remembered."

"James dear, we should go change before our lecture on environmentalism and skiing." They stood to leave and we said goodbye.

Once they were gone, Porsche turned to me, "What do you think of that? Could that Christopher guy be the link between them?"

"Christopher Burns. Sure, at this point anything is possible. But that was second hand and he claimed the poker guy wasn't sure anyway. If the ski instructor was flirting with her, perhaps Christopher was too. After the argument with his wife, so he could've been drinking and flirted a bit before staying in the library the rest of the night. I don't know, but we'll pass it along to Johan."

We stayed there for a while soaking up the fire's warmth and extending the spa experience as long as we could. We had some of the complimentary tea and watched the windows shimmer from the sun making an anemic appearance in the sky. The worst was over, at least I hoped so.

We went to our room to change. I checked on the raccoons only to find they had vacated the balcony. The blanket was left in a pile, but all scraps of food we had slipped them was nowhere in evidence. Maybe the worst of the weather was truly over and our little refugees sensed it and left.

I showered and put on jeans and a cashmere sweater. The conference was done, so I could dress more casual. I hadn't brought many extra clothes, not like Porsche. The sunlight, frail as it was, had lightened my mood so I put on some dangle pearl earrings and a long pearl necklace for a touch of chic. Porsche and I were ready to join the hubbub again, albeit reluctantly.

Porsche and I were in the lobby on the way to our lunch reservation, when we couldn't help but overhear a couple at the front desk.

"The roads are clearing. We want to leave now, you can't hold us hostage here," The burly husband said, not quite yelling but close.

The soft-spoken wife attempted to mitigate her husband's angry words. "Not that you haven't done your best in a bad situation dear. We just really have to go home now."

"Porsche, call Johan now. This could get out of hand." She hadn't seen the near riot the other day. But, I had and didn't want a repeat performance of that scene.

Chapter Twenty

I approached the couple in hopes of softening the potentially riotous problem if others heard and joined the push to leave.

"I couldn't help but overhear. It's great news about the weather letting up and the roads will be opening soon but they weren't open the last I heard? You won't get far. Besides, I thought we were also providing the police time to investigate." I was trying to channel my mother's voice to reason with an unruly child. I knew it so well.

"I would think they've had plenty of time by now…" He began.

"Oh, even with all the wrecks and emergencies that took resources away from the investigation? It's not as though this was the only problem the police had to deal with." Leading them by the hand.

"Oh dear, I hadn't thought of that." The wife said. Her eyebrows carved into a deep "v" shape. Hubby still had a bullish look on his face.

"I can't help it they didn't get the investigation done yet. They can't expect me to stay, I'm not going to pay for a single day past my scheduled check out."

I looked at the front desk clerk. Her big eyes and open mouth told me she didn't know the answer to that demand either. I was about to suggest she call the manager or assistant when Johan arrived. He'd rushed to the lobby and skidded to a stop at our little group.

"Oh good. Detective Larson, perhaps you can give us an update on the investigation and road conditions. This couple is anxious to leave." I figured he would understand the situation with that introduction.

Johan nodded curtly. "I've been in touch with state officials and we would appreciate everybody staying through today." He had drawn himself up to his full height and puffed his chest out like a rooster. But the irate man had his hands on his hips.

It was a showdown and I felt like we could have slipped back in time with the sheriff having a standoff with a ruffian. I cracked a smile in spite of how serious the situation could potentially get.

"You can't just keep us here against our will." The man huffed.

"I appreciate how you likely want to get home. Give us one more day to investigate. We have your home address and information correct?" Johan was pouring on the charm now. I wondered how he probably used that tool more often in his job than any other.

The husband looked at his wife, "What do you say, dear?"

"I guess we can stay one more day, but then I really want to get home to my little princess." The lady answered. "My poodle." She added by way of explanation.

One crisis averted. We were down to hours before the killer would return home. Mere short hours remained until the chances of solving the case or arresting the killer diminished before he or she was loose to potentially leave the country.

The couple turned and meandered to the elevator. The front desk lady looked a bit shell-shocked still but gave us a weak smile.

"We were headed for lunch and I heard them. I didn't want another uprising." I explained.

Johan's eyes were still red with bags under his eyes. His hair was limp and I suspected he hadn't shaved yet today from the accumulated growth.

"Mind if I join you for lunch, I may not eat otherwise." He looked at me but I wasn't sure he even focused.

"If you um, don't mind sitting with Porsche." I wasn't sure how he might feel about that on top of his dilemma with two murders to solve. I motioned towards her standing by the staircase

"Yeah, okay. I know it's a little awkward, but we had a good talk last night."

Okaaaaay, but I worried how Porsche might feel about my inviting him without consulting her first.

Johan walked over to Porsche, "Thanks for the call. I know keeping everyone together can't last much longer." He took a deep breath. "Would you mind if I joined you and Julienne for lunch? It'll give me a chance to catch my breath and eat." They both looked uncomfortable and didn't make eye contact.

We were in the little café, Mountain Chalet, in a corner slightly away from the main traffic. There was actually some sunshine glinting on the windows occasionally. I hadn't realized how subdued I felt with all the gray and gloom until just a glimpse of sun warmed my spirits and brought a smile to my face. As much as I was enjoying the resort and restaurants, I was looking forward to being home.

I looked at the menu and still wanted a home-cooked meal. I would kill for some homemade meatloaf. Don't get me wrong, the Bavarian and German dishes had been amazing, but the menu didn't have anything I really wanted to try anymore.

We placed our orders and jumped right into the problem at hand.

"Do we really get to leave tomorrow?" I tried to wait as long as I could, but I ended up just blurting it out.

"I'm afraid so. I don't have enough to hold my persons of interest, all forensics have been collected, all staff and guests have been questioned twice now, and the two victim's rooms remain empty and preserved. Once the roads are safe, I really can't force every guest to incur more expense and stay indefinitely." He took several swallows of the coffee the waitress had brought. "So unless more evidence is discovered or this is somehow blown wide open, we'll be relying on the forensic evidence going to Denver labs. There's a chance they may find something, but that could take weeks, maybe even months." His shoulders slumped.

Porsche placed a hand on his arm. "You've worked hard and done your best in extenuating circumstances. That's all anybody can expect." He reflexively placed his hand over hers.

"I got something from the massage therapist this morning." I took a drink from my coffee. Oh, I would miss this dark brew though. "Leona was upset that her boyfriend made it here but with his wife. Get this, it was even some sort of anniversary which made it worse. So, she was having a long-running affair."

Porsche jumped in, "So that ruby necklace from her boyfriend could have been a gift from a married man. If the married guy killed her, then it makes sense he would take the necklace on the chance he could be linked to purchasing such an expensive gift." Well yes, that made sense. *Why didn't I think of that?*

We stopped talking while the waitress delivered our meals and we each took a bite.

Johan picked up the conversation. "That would explain why the sim card from her cell phone was removed too. Any text or phone calls to and from the married man would incriminate him." Either the coffee was reviving him, or he functioned well with little sleep because I missed that rather obvious connection.

"There's the possibility of a wife killing her too. If the wife was enraged, I bet she could strangle Leona. Particularly if she had the element of surprise." Porsche chimed in.

Johan was making notes in his notepad. I gave him a few moments to catch up before I continued.

"Plus, the massage therapist who treated Kara Thursday shared with my therapist that Kara was excited about getting even with someone or exposing something. No names." I waited for him to write that down.

"After our massages, we sat in the lounge around the fire and Porsche gossiped with an older couple who had another tidbit." I motioned for Porsche to relay her information.

"Well, apparently the man heard from a poker player last night..." At Johan's raised eyebrows and obvious doubt already she stopped. "Okay, I know that sounds convoluted, but it's no worse than third hand through the therapist grapevine. So anyway, the man shared he saw Leona with that Chris guy, the one suing Kara. He said Chris was pretty close to Leona and cozy. Maybe he is her lover and he got away from his wife for a few moments."

Johan stopped taking notes, "I just wish all these people would've come to the police when they heard or saw things concerning this case."

I didn't know what to say so I took another bite of my sandwich. My theory was people would gossip over things that might be salacious or odd but they wouldn't consider it actually criminal or important enough to report to the police. We lapsed into quiet as we each devoted our energy to eating.

We each finished in record time and the uncomfortable silence had stretched long enough.

"Okay guys, I'm going to my room and Skype with family." I didn't want to say I would be devoting my time to internet research on the suspects. Johan may not appreciate the assistance. I also wanted to consult with my original investigative assistants, my neighbors at Mountain Shadows.

I stood up only to see the young man, Justin, at the entryway looking around. I sat back down and shifted so Johan blocked any view of me.

"What...?" Porsche started but saw Justin looking around. "Is that the kid who is crushing on you?" She had a wicked twinkle in her eyes.

"Don't you dare call him over here, I'll never forgive you...and his future therapist visits will be on your head." My whisper didn't come out as lethal as I planned.

Johan moved to turn around and look, but I grabbed his arm. "Aren't you supposed to protect and aid those in need? Then don't turn around or move. I am not going to trample that boy's ego." I sounded desperate. Okay, maybe I was a little.

He turned to Porsche, "How old is this kid?"

"Oh, fifteen or sixteen." She guessed.

Johan chuckled, "His ego will be hurt for a little while until a girl his age strikes his fancy and then you will be a memory he dreams of when he's having his mid-life crisis years from now." That was good news for Justin and left me feeling...replaceable.

Justin finally gave up and left. He was determined; I'd give him that.   I waited another minute and left the restaurant.   To avoid Justin, I sprinted up the grand staircase like dogs were chasing me and skidded to a halt to show my identification to the hall monitor.

In my room, I put on some decaf coffee to brew and turned on my laptop. I settled in and had just entered Preston the realtor to Google when my Skype popped up. I know I was supposed to be chatting with family, but I wasn't telling Detective Larson I was doing some internet investigating.

My neighbor Nathan's aged face appeared, filling the screen as he was too close to the web camera. Nathan was a retired doctor with long white hair usually tied back in a ponytail.

"Hey, young lady, glad I caught you..." He began

"You're too close, don't you know how to do this?" I could hear the disembodied voice of my other neighbor Delores. "See where I'm pointing ya ole goat. That's your big nose filling the camera. Sit back, don't give the girl a view of your nose hairs." She continued to mutter in the background.

He backed away but only slightly. "Domineering Delores is on my case as you can hear." He smiled a tobacco-stained grin.

Auburn shorthaired Delores began shouldering him over, "Move your old bones over so I can chat with her too. Don't hog the camera." She was a regular at Skyping with her grandchildren. Beverly managed to get both of them in the camera frame.

"We're glad to catch you, dear. We heard a news report that the local realtor Kara Caine died in Vail. You wouldn't happen to know anything about that, would you?" Her eyebrows were raised in question. I guess the police couldn't keep it out of the news for long with all the resort guests talking to family and friends.

"Ummm, yes and no. She was staying here but I really didn't know her." Although they had been my original Baker Street Irregulars last fall without even realizing that's what they were, I didn't want to dance around and I wasn't sure how much I was allowed to share.

"Oh dear, Julie is holding out on us. Do you believe that?" Nathan shook his head.

"She knows more than she's sharing, I can see it in her eyes." Delores always thought she could read people... okay, she thought she could read me. She was usually correct. I don't know how she did it either.

"You think you're so smart, but just maybe you're wrong." Nathan tossed out the challenge.

"Look guys, it's an ongoing investigation..." *I probably shouldn't have said that.*

"See, told you."

"Bet we can help." Nathan was quick to add.

Chapter Twenty-one

"I don't know how you could help, we have only a few hours before all the guests are released tomorrow and odds of arrest after that will diminish."

"Let this be a lesson to you girl, you should've gotten with us sooner and we could've had this all cleared up by now." Nathan wore his disappointed look. He had grown children so I got the benefit of his years of looks and guilt trips he had honed with his kids in his arsenal against me. I didn't have a chance.

"I'm not involved, I was nowhere near the woman and I didn't discover the body either. So I don't know what you expect from me."

Beverly moved her face closer giving a close-up of her wrinkled face, "Don't try to bamboozle us. We know you probably have a finger on what's happening. We want to help you, dear."

"Help me? I don't see how guys."

"We might have some insights. Anybody local involved that we might know?" Nathan had a glint in his eyes.

I debated if I should share the few suspect names. There was a chance they might have come across one or more of them since they were involved in the community.

I shared the people I would like to know more about and provided an overview of motives for each. They were like giddy children writing down the names.

"I can tell you right now Kara would go to City Council meetings and stir the pot. Sometimes she would seem reasonable until you saw her away from a microphone. I witnessed her get dogged mean if she didn't like a person or their proposals." Beverly would go to City Council meetings fairly regularly to keep busy. I suspected she gave council members her two cents as well.

Nathan had been busy typing away, "I thought that name sounded familiar. Preston Pinder is a realtor I know a bit. He's had several bad deals with Caine and warns people away from dealing with her. They've had bad blood for a while now. I think they even had a professional mediation to resolve one deal. Wish I had more on him."

"Wait a minute, what was that gal's name again?" Beverly asked.

"Debra Graham, she's self-employed with her own grant writing business and volunteers." I had got that from online research already.

Beverly's forehead was wrinkled in concentration "I think I know her, drinks like a fish." I choked in surprise; Beverly, the tattooed short dynamo with a southern accent, could out drink most anybody. "I remember there was a rumor I'd dismissed at the time, that her husband left her for being emotionally unstable. Of course, that's a rumor and I have no evidence of any such condition."

I had considered Debra as my least likely suspect, but I thought about her some more. Revenge is a powerful motivation and she has certainly let her anger fester. From the visit to the gym that morning we witnessed she was strong enough to maneuver dead weight, maybe not like tossing a bag of potatoes, but she could probably manage. But what would she honestly have against Leona?

"Hey guys, what do you know about Leona Dolman?" I didn't bother to share that she was another victim. Currently, they were happy to help but that could change to overprotective in a heartbeat and they would have my aunt and uncle in a tizzy.

"Doesn't ring a bell at all."

Well, I at least learned that realtor Preston has had long running issues with Kara. I wasn't counting on the dubious rumors about Debra as true, although she certainly knew how to hold a grudge.

Beverly patted her gray hair, "Are there many single men there? I love a man who fills out a cable knit sweater." Her eyes had a sparkle.

Nathan swatted at her. "She wouldn't notice single guys, she's taken." I didn't want to tip them off concerning my reservations about my couple status. I was fairly sure after his latest bodyguard job and lack of communication, I would break up with Mason. This time away had given me some clarity about what I truly wanted and needed from a man.

"Oh please, like every guy doesn't notice women even if they're married. I call BS. Women get to look too." She winked at the camera and I chuckled. My senior neighbors were a handful and I missed them.

We chatted for a few more minutes and caught up on events at Mountain Shadows, the townhome complex where I lived. Colorado Springs had only gotten a few inches from the storm at a little over six thousand feet elevation, not like Vail got socked.

I described the events to keep us all busy and occupied, knowing they would find it interesting.

Beverly had a wicked gleam in her eye. "But do they have a nude painting class with a live male model? I wouldn't even drink during that painting class." Nathan sputtered at that. Beverly was incorrigible.

I said goodbye to the terrible twosome. I had just finished clearing out my email when Porsche breezed into our room.

"We have to get ready for tonight, come on."

I stared at her, "It's not for...almost two hours yet. I only need a few minutes."

"Oh no you don't. We are getting dressed up tonight and having our hair done. I made us appointments." She smiled like I should reward her, as if.

"Have you and Felicia made an alliance against me?" My cousin Felicia was usually the one trying to dress me like a life-size doll.

"I do believe it was you just the other day who dressed up for dinner by yourself.   Let me think." She placed two fingers to her chin and looked off into space, "Yes, that was definitely you getting all spiffed up. This is a masked party and probably the most fun we'll have this entire fiasco. Humor me. Okay?"

I hated it when she did that.   "Fine, but don't go overboard. This isn't that big of a deal."

Porsche had opened the small closet and began taking out dresses she had brought. I now understood why she had brought two large suitcases.   She had claimed sweaters were bulky, but she had a full contingent of clothes for most occasions.

I, on the other hand, had only brought clothes appropriate for the conference and maintaining a business persona with a few pairs of jeans and winter sweaters added.

"Here, try these on and let me see." She handed me five dresses.

It was useless to fight it…resistance was futile applied in this case. I tried on the first dress, a clingy knit maroon color number. I took my phone and got the oldies song *I'm Too Sexy* to play as I walked out as if I was a model on the catwalk. I held my head up, adopted a serious look into the distance, and strut to the patio door, spun and faced Porsche with my hands on my hips.

She applauded and laughed. "Next one."

I repeated my performance to another runway-worthy tune.

"Work it, honey." She said between laughing.

We repeated the catwalk with various songs until she settled on a plum-colored raw silk dress with oriental styling and long skirt with a split. Naturally, she had shoes to coordinate. I was of average height, but with the shoes I looked long-legged and sleek even. I had to admit some long gloves would've made me feel like Audrey Hepburn, my favorite actress. *The chicken dance was out tonight.*

She eventually settled on a sexy and playful sleeveless red dress with a full skirt and matching heels for herself. She informed me we were due at the spa for hair and makeup and we grabbed some glitzy clutch purses.

I had never had my hair and makeup done by professionals. I explained I didn't like heavy makeup to my *artiste*. She studied me, shifting my head for every angle. "I'm thinking of putting your hair up, if you are agreeable."

"Okay, let's do it." I rarely put my hair up, so this would be an experience.

After my hair was washed, blown out, and put in spiral curlers, she began on my makeup. I was facing away from the mirror so I couldn't see what she was doing. She was quiet, her complete attention on what she was doing.

What felt like half an hour later she finished with makeup and removed the curlers. She quietly explained what she was doing for the hairstyle while she worked. She took the crown section of my hair and worked in sections, hair spraying and then back brushing to build a full top. She then twisted it and created a slight poof of hair and tucked the ends under the back with bobby pins. The rest of the hair she loosely wrapped strips around several fingers and then pinned the sculpted rings around the back of my head and nape of my neck. She draped the curls on the sides and fixed them with more pins.

When I finally got to look in a hand mirror, I was amazed. It was the most romantic updo I had ever seen. It was worthy of a fantasy princess. Then I saw the makeup. I smiled. Even though it felt like I had a lot of makeup, it didn't look like it. My eyes stood out but the overall look was soft and dreamy.

Porsche squealed when she saw me. She opened her purse and took out a pair of rhinestone drop earrings for me and gold chandelier for her.

I turned to my hair and makeup guru and hugged her. "Can you take a picture of us please?"

We posed in front of the spa's glass entry doors with the resort name on the glass. I got the picture I wanted with Porsche even though it wasn't outdoors in the snow.

"I'm posting this on Facebook and tagging Mason. I don't think he's ever seen you looking this stunning, so it's my duty to show him what he's missing." She gave me a big smile and winked. The photo was my equivalent of his red carpet photo. Probably the closest I'd come.

It was time for the masked party and I had a suspicion we were definitely overdressed. Porsche handed me a mask, one of the feathered ones she had grabbed from the creepy wall. We put them on and were amazed at how such a small item could add mystery.

All of the meeting rooms we had used for the conference had the walls removed so it was one large ballroom. To one side I could see a long buffet table and the desserts were set apart for traffic flow. We signed in by our room numbers so they would charge dinner to our room to make it easy.

Smaller tables were scattered around with lovely candles on mirrors for centerpieces. The overhead chandeliers were dimmed to a soft glow. Twinkle lights adorned potted silk trees all around and walls had sheer golden fabric draped for lush backdrops. The sound system had jazz music playing and the overall feel was of an upscale carnival.

My worries that we were overdressed were unfounded. News of being able to leave tomorrow gave this a buoyant party feel and most people were wearing their dressy best. We decided to just enjoy the evening and put the murders out of our thoughts. I could do it – really. We headed to the cash bar and stood in line waiting to order something to put us in a more festive mood.

Of course, all the suspects had to parade in front of me at that moment, testing my resolve. Debra wore an emerald green pantsuit and held her leopard spotted mask in her hand.

Preston and his wife strolled by arm in arm. He wore slacks and button down shirt with a wool blazer while his wife had a lovely dress with a slight sprinkling of sequins. She had her mask on, a red and gold harlequin design.

Preston held his mask, matching hers only with black and gold diamonds.

Bryce was alone as his girlfriend never returned after their fight *the* first deadly night. He wore slacks and a nice red sweater. I watched him slip on his basic and simple mask with swirled colors of teal and white with braided ribbon edging.

Lawsuit Christopher and his wife with their son in tow passed my field of vision a little further away. She wore a basic black dress and he had on a smoky gray blazer over a hunter green sweater with black jeans. I didn't see a mask in evidence for any of their party.

I was next to place an order and after a few questions I ordered a cranberry zombie that was supposed to be like a rum punch. I was sipping on my drink and waiting for Porsche to get her chocolate martini.

Wade and his wife were fashionably late and waving to a few people they knew or had gotten to know while here. He was in a dark button-down shirt with dress black slacks. He had his mask pushed up to rest on the top of his head. His wife was wearing a big smile, an expensive looking tea-length silver dress, and a silky smooth bun with a rhinestone barrette or comb accent. She was an older version of Hepburn in Breakfast at Tiffany's, minus the long black gloves.

Porsche got her drink and we made our way through the people standing, weaving around groups chatting. The first open seats together we sat down to claim. Even without a live band, a few were on the dance floor to a slow song playing over the sound system. Combined with the spa treatment this felt like a special occasion.

"I'm going to check out the buffet," Porsche announced.

"I'll keep our seats safe." I offered since they were a rare item.

I sat sipping my drink and felt some mental tension slip away. I had been so wrapped up in the conference which was overwhelming at times with the fire hose of information, the murder and multiple suspects, Porsche's new relationship vulnerability, and of course Mason posing as somebody else's boyfriend. I was enjoying just watching people dance and let my mind wander.

I didn't even see him sneak up. Justin sat in Porsche's chair and leaned toward me.

Chapter Twenty-two

"I've been looking for you. I was afraid I wouldn't recognize you if you wore a mask." Apparently, he was happy to have tracked me down. *Oh goody.*

What good were these masks if you could still recognize a person? What to do now?

"Hello, am I interrupting?" Tammy stood behind Justin.

"Tammy, of course not. Please join us, Porsche just went to the buffet." I was so happy to see her. I was sending a desperate message with my eyes pleading *don't leave me.* I took off my mask so she could see my pleading eyes better.

Justin cleared his throat, uncomfortable with so many adults no doubt. "Would you like to dance?" He asked with a hopeful look. Oh, why me? I looked between him and Tammy and swallowed.

"I'd be delighted to dance with you young man," Tammy offered, "but I don't' think her boyfriend would approve." She winked for my benefit.

"I think your boyfriend isn't real. I found out you're here with your friend. What guy lets his girl go to a romantic resort without him?" He looked at me with an open and earnest appeal.

Good question. He didn't know the half of it!

"Um, well it's never that simple," was all I could manage.

His eyes shifted to what I guessed were his parents waving for him to join them, "I'll be back and maybe we can dance later." He left and I let out my breath.

"That is one determined boy who's smitten with you." Tammy chuckled as she sat in Porsche's seat.

I groaned, "I'm too young to be a cougar and besides, I should be able to attract eligible men my own age." Eligible, meaning emotionally available as well as my age – thank you very much!

"You have a boyfriend I thought." She looked concerned.

That peaceful relaxed feeling flew out the proverbial window. I took out my cell phone from the glitzy little purse and pulled up the photo of Mason on the red carpet he sent me. He wore an expensive suit, which he looks particularly good in. His rugged good looks combined with naturally wavy shoulder-length hair and broad shoulders were a potent mix.

I explained, "That's him, he sent that in a text. He's…in California for work."

"Wish you were here. Hmmmm. What does he do that takes him to the red carpet without you?" Her eyebrows had pinched together.

If it weren't for the text, most people probably wouldn't even believe I actually knew him let alone he was my guy. I felt like I had to prove I wasn't lying.

"I know it seems unbelievable, but he occasionally does bodyguard work for celebrities." The words were incredible, but I also felt like he wouldn't want me sharing that much since he works *undercover* as their boyfriend.

Of course, I could just be an idiot and believe some outlandish tale he fed me when he is still a full-blown playboy. I thought the man I trusted last fall was earnest with me, but I could've been wrong. I just didn't know him well enough to be sure.

"He seems familiar, is he famous?" Her eyes scrutinized me.

"He's a photographer, and he has done the bodyguard thing for a while so he may be in some celebrity photos." Okay, probably a whole bunch of photos. I felt totally stupid. I was tensing up with every word.

Her eyes changed to sympathetic. "This is a sore spot and I'm making it worse. I'm sorry dear."

I waved her comment off. I didn't want to talk about my angst over Mason especially with the noise level rising and my nearly yelling. Porsche returned and I let her take my seat and made my way to the buffet, away from talking about my kinda-sorta boyfriend.

I progressed down the food line, recognizing the same offerings served for some of the conference luncheons. The many entrées and side dishes mingled into a heady aroma that had my stomach growl in anticipation. The occasional strong perfume from a fellow guest would overpower the food. I absently placed items on my plate when a conversation broke through my fog.

"I'm so excited to be going home tomorrow. I might not even take a sleeping pill to sleep tonight." Mrs. Lochran was commenting to a lady next to her.

"Oh, I sleep like a rock no matter what. Always have." The unknown lady answered.

"Wade is so good and made sure I was getting good sleep. He fusses over me. I'm not complaining, it's better than the alternative." She mused.

Better than the alternative... like Mason – emotionally distant? Our first few months was littered with indications he wasn't ready for commitment, but I accepted the excuses. I could see that looking back now. After the discussion with Tammy, I couldn't help but go there. I shook my head and focused on what I was piling on my plate.

By the time I returned to the table, Johan had joined our group and somehow we now had extra chairs crowded around the table. Perhaps being the police he got a few favors.

Porsche was reserved chatting with him, but she had an air of bittersweet joy. I ached for her. It was all enough to make me swear off romance movies, let alone dating.

Tammy made a trip to load up with food too and for a while, conversation came to a halt while our collective focus was on eating and people watching. That didn't last long though.

Tammy jumped into the taboo subject of the night, the proverbial elephant in the room. "All our prime suspects are in one place. I don't suppose there is a dramatic arrest to take place detective?"

Johan shook his head and sighed, "I wish that were the case. I have to say, I take all the guests disbanding and scattering to their respective homes as a personal defeat." His eyes were surrounded by deep worry lines.

"You can't blame yourself, it was a confluence of events." Porsche offered.

The thought of a killer getting away galled me too, I understood – on a much smaller scale no doubt – how Johan must feel.

Porsche and Tammy got up to choose a dessert, leaving me alone with the detective.

"I want to thank you for funneling information to me the last few days. I wish I hadn't involved you."

"Don't worry about that, it's the least I could do. I wish I could've been more useful actually." I confided.

"I don't understand why more people didn't share openly when I questioned them." He shook his head.

"Oh, I suppose it is a few things. The person really may not see any significance in what they saw or heard so they don't want to get a person in trouble over nothing. Perhaps it is so insignificant that they don't even remember it at all.

Or, the idea of coming close to a brush with death just from seeing or hearing something pushes it from the mind as self-preservation." I offered a few of my own conclusions over the same question.

He sat, sipping his club soda and lime, looking at Porsche. "I never expected to find her in the midst of this investigation.   You were correct to warn me of the temporary nature. Still, I..." His thought trailed off.

When Porsche and Tammy sat back down I decided to cruise the dessert table myself.   I was staring at the selections, all decedent and works of art.   My mind wondered to a flurry of thoughts jumbled together. A tap on the shoulder sent my thoughts flying out of my head.

"May I have this dance?" Justin had snuck up on me. I cursed my luck. But he wasn't going to stop and maybe just one dance and I could send him on his way.

The music mix that played on the sound system alternated between energetic dance tunes and slow romantic selections. Currently, it was a fun toe-tapping song. But as soon as we started to dance, the song ended and – you guessed it, a slow song began playing. I think it was the theme to the movie Romeo and Juliet. *Just my luck.*

Justin blushed and tried to take me in his arms, I extended my right hand and placed my left on his shoulder for a traditional couple dance pose, even if we only managed a side step. Justin swallowed and his eyes took on an anxious look.

His hand came around too low on my back and I moved it up to my shoulder. "I guess you get to learn how to dance. "

"I know how to dance, just not like this."

"Trust me, this will impress girls as you get older." I wasn't actually sure on that score. I got him to do a basic side-touch step. Then got him to do a turn as he did the side touch. By the end of the dance, he was beaming.

"That wasn't so bad, was it?"

"It was easy once I got my feet to cooperate." He flashed a shy smile.

"Why don't you practice with your mother, that would be special for her."

He was disappointed when I left the dance floor and returned to my seat, but he did bring his mother out to dance for the next slow song. He flashed a smile in my direction at the end of the dance. I suspected he would sweep some girl off her feet in the near future with that simple dance step.

"That was nice of you to teach him to dance," Tammy commented next to me.

"Purely ulterior motives of self-preservation. It kept him from getting too comfortable and made it more formal."

"Maybe they should've given some dance lessons for an activity." She commented and I nodded.

By the next slow dance, Justin was back. This time Johan asked Porsche to dance too.

We all joined the dance floor that was now getting crowded as more people joined the fun. I explained how he had to lead through the minefield and keep us from colliding with other couples. We had only a few mishaps.

Wade Lochran and his wife were close and my eyes fixed on the cuff of his shirt on the extended hand holding his wife's hand. His hunter green button down shirt cuff had two clear buttons rather than matching dark green like the others as if they were replacement buttons from a travel sewing kit.

My mind flashed to a vision of him that first night in the bar when I met him. He had on that bright pistachio colored sweater and that same shirt under it.

Could it be?

Chapter Twenty-three

I ignored Justin and danced on while thinking. Could the yarn and button found with Kara be from Wade's sweater and shirt? Several people had worn green shirts and sweaters. It was popular with the men, I'd even seen Debra wearing green. If Kara was going to expose something, as the front desk person had overheard, what would she reveal about him? What would he have killed Leona over?

I remembered Leona was staying down the hall from Wade. Could she have seen him leave or return to his room the night Kara was killed? Of course, Wade saw her talking to Johan and a few hours later she was dead. He might have feared she would tell what she knew.

But Wade had his wife as an alibi. They were both asleep. But...

I had been watching Wade on the dance floor as the song continued. Our eyes locked for several seconds. I saw the recognition in his eyes that I suspected him with more than a theory. I think I understood how he killed Kara and even Leona. The details on exactly why were a little fuzzy still. His eyes flitted around the room. Looking for where the detective was maybe? He began leading his wife through the crowded dance floor in our direction.

"Justin, I need you to do me a favor. You need to find the detective and tell him I know who the killer is. Do you understand?" My voice must have revealed more than I wanted.

"Yeah, okay. Where're you going to be?"

"Hopefully away from here and a potential hostage situation. Go. Now." He let go of me and left the dance floor into the main room. I couldn't say if Wade was desperate enough to take hostages, but I definitely thought he was desperate enough to have killed twice already. I had to keep the guests safe at least.

I walked down the center of the ballroom as quickly as I could. I didn't see Tammy or Porsche around, let alone Johan. I stopped several feet before the entrance doors. If he was going to push the issue, I hoped somebody would witness I'd left with him.

I glanced back and he was approaching fast. I took out my phone and dialed Porsche, I didn't even have time to text. I left the phone in my hand hoping he wouldn't notice.

"Wade, why are you following me?" I wanted to make sure the phone picked up the conversation. I prayed Porsche could hear the phone over the party noise or it hadn't gone to voicemail. *Where was she?*

"We need to take a little walk young lady and I won't take no for an answer." His voice was low, oozing malice. He grabbed my arm in a vicious grip and jerked me toward the door.

"Wade, stop you're hurting me. You don't want to hurt me, please." All for the phone's sake and to maybe talk him down. Mason had begun teaching me some self-defense, but that was mostly how to break out of chokeholds.

"Where's your wife? Maybe we should all sit down and talk because this has to be a misunderstanding." *Where the hell was Porsche, and more importantly Johan. Had Justin found him?*

"Leave my wife out of this. You loose sleazy women running around. You could learn from her. She knows her place, in the home raising children and obeying. This country has suffered enough from the likes of you." He spat out.

I had never read any of his editorials, but that seemed one of his typical topics somebody had mentioned. He threw the exit door open and jerked my arm again. I yelped as pain exploded through my shoulder and I feared he would dislodge my arm from the socket if he jerked it again.

I wanted to stay quiet to avoid further injury to my shoulder but I needed to keep the phone line updated as best I could. I was trotting to keep up so he didn't jerk. We were at the spa, empty and dark now. It had a feeling of desertion.

"The spa? Why..."

He slapped me so hard my head slammed to the side and pain exploded near my left eye. For some irrational reason, a line from the movie *Pretty Woman* ran through my head when Vivian asked if boys were taught how to slap girls in high school.

That. Was. It. I took my arm and twisted it towards his thumb in a fast and equally vicious move hoping I'd broke his thumb. The move shot pain through my shoulder. Although my arm was free he blocked any escape.

There was no use in pretending I didn't know. "Why? What happened that you would kill Kara?"

"That vile witch didn't know her place either. How dare she presume to correct me on my behavior. I'm a man of faith and she was a godless witch. She had the gall to try and expose me. Me!"

Okay, score one for the gossip, she was going to expose somebody. Reading between the lines, it was definitely something he did.

"What could've been so bad to warrant killing her? You could've faced whatever it was." I used rational thought to get him to settle down.

He looked at me as if speaking to a simpleton. "I'm a pillar of the community and the taint of an affair, well, people wouldn't understand. I'd lose credibility, influence, my standing as a leader."

I had heard how he was big into his church and influenced political figures with his views, he and his wife even had some involvement in more politicized teaching materials they were trying to get schools to use as curriculum. News of an affair would be a scandal – of sorts, but anymore it barely raised eyebrows because it was so commonplace.

From what little I had seen and heard of Kara, she would throw in his face how she discovered his indiscretion – his hypocrisy – and how she planned to go public. If she had just kept her mouth shut, she might still be alive. I couldn't understand that need to push a person.

"Did Leona see you, try and blackmail you maybe?"

He let out a hollow laugh, "She was my mistress for several years. That's why her room was so close, so I could visit easily day or night." He watched the surprise on my face. "Don't let that shock you, I had more varied needs that she satisfied. More, shall we say, vigorous and specific needs that she excelled in satisfying."

Well, shut my mouth, literally. I wasn't going to ask him, didn't want to know the details on that one anyway. Hey, he called me loose when he had a mistress.

"You killed your mistress too?" I blurted out as the significance sank fully into my thoughts. I really hoped somebody was getting all this on the phone. Where was Johan?

"Leona served a need, scratched an itch. It was fine as long as she knew her place, on her back or on her knees. She dared to get angry that my wife joined me when it was none of her business. Then she had the gall to threaten to tell the police I killed Kara. The little whore acted like she was better than me." His eyes were soulless but his voice was saturated with disgust.

Other than being a cold-blooded killer, he was without any compassion...lacking in any devotion or love that he put his mistress a few hundred feet away so he could leave his wife in bed and slip out to be with the other. No true feelings for either woman.

He swiftly grabbed my hair gathered and pinned up at the back of my head and jerked my head close to him. Dang, he was lightning fast.

"I tried to warn you off in the hallway the other night. I guess you need to be taught a lesson in person. Typical rebellious woman – you should have a man keeping you in line." I kept my mouth shut, no time to counter his antiquated attitude.

His face was twisted into an ugly snarling visage. I had to find a way out of this. I took the heal of my hand from my undamaged arm and punched with all my might at the bridge of his nose. Thank you self-defense video I had watched online intended to break the nose and inflict pain.

He howled, from pain or rage. Blood was running from his nose. I took my high heels off and had one in each hand with the spiked heels facing him and backed away toward the party where my chances of Johan finding me increased. Lochran charged me and I braced myself.

When he got close and grabbed me by the throat I began striking his arms with the sharp heals as hard as I could, then moved to strike at his face. He had to remove a hand to protect his face. With his free hand, he grabbed a shoe, and I struck him in the face with my other heal.

"Freeze, police!" I couldn't tell if it was Johan or not because I was fading to black for the second time at this resort. *Crap. Just crap.*

I opened my eyes again and found myself in the spa on a treatment table with people crowded around me.

"How long....?" My throat closed shut. It felt like a metal cheese grater had scraped my throat raw. I remembered Wade choking me and gently felt my throat. Yep, it was still there between my head and shoulders, tender in places. I would have spectacular bruises tomorrow on my throat and face where he struck me.

"Only five minutes or so hun." Tammy, on my right, said.

Porsche, to my left, explained. "Justin got Johan and they found you fighting with him. Lockran was losing that fight anyway from the looks of it. His face is worse for having tangled with you."

With their help, I sat up on the side of the treatment table and they each hopped up to sit on either side to prop me up. Kylie and Zack were standing just inside the door with anxious looks pinching their faces.

"I'm...fine." I pointed to my throat, "Hurts a little." I sounded as bad as it felt.

Justin ran up to the door with a glass of water and a blue ice pack. Both felt so good on my throat. I smiled at him and he beamed.

"Pen...paper," I whispered and made little writing motions.

Kylie and Zack ran through the spa and returned with some printer paper and a pen.

I wrote out how Lochran had confessed he killed Kara because she was going to expose his hypocritical extramarital affair. Then he killed his mistress of several years. Although he didn't say, I think Leona was finished with satisfying his darker desires when he brought his wife along on their *anniversary* of some sort. When I observed Leona over dinner, she had looked at Wade and his wife in a more appraisal than jealous or loving way.

Porsche and Tammy read along as I wrote it out, I handed the paper to the others and they gathered around to read it.

Kylie shook her head and looked ready to cry, tears poised to flow but she held them back. It could have become a maudlin group, but Johan walked in at that moment.

"I need a few minutes with her please." Everybody deserted me pronto.

I handed him the paper I had started. After reading it, he looked at me with laser eyes.

"Did you go off on your own? Because that was a serious risk." Constrained anger reverberated off him.

I wrote on the paper how I was dancing when I saw his buttons and got to thinking, then Wade Lochran looked at me and he could see the truth. I didn't know what he might do in a crowd so I wanted to remove that risk and sent Justin to get him.

He read my reply and his shoulders relaxed a bit and I no longer felt he would combust from being mad at me.

"Calling Porsche and mentioning the spa helped. I got there as soon as I could." His voice was gentle and laced with regret.

I wrote *not your fault* out on the paper for him. There was a knock on the door and Johan talked with the person for a few moments then turned.

"This is the doctor, I think you two met a few days ago." *Gee, how could I forget?*

I lifted a hand and wiggled my fingers in a wave.

Johan let Porsche come in during my exam, but he returned to hear the verdict.

"Her throat is swollen from the choking but should be fine in a few days. The bruise starting around her left eye will look bad, but I don't think there is any serious damage. Her shoulder took some abuse." He took a pillowcase off a spa pillow and folded it to use as a sling for my arm.

"I'll have an actual sling delivered first thing in the morning but use the pillowcase for now. You must wear a sling for at least a week to let all the tendons and muscles heal. When you're home, your physician will want to do an MRI on the shoulder and an x-ray of your skull and neck because your head has had two blows. He needs to determine what your treatment should involve once your home." He wrote it all down and handed Porsche the directions.

"I'll make sure she does it."

I was released to my room and I stood to make the trek when Johan actually swept me off my feet and began carrying me, careful to keep my tender shoulder from door jams. It was kind but made me miss Mason even more. It was the sort of move he would have done.

Settled into my room and bed, Porsche got ice and used the towel again for a new cold compress on my shoulder, I still had the original reusable ice pack around my neck. She also dissolved one of the pain pills the doctor gave her in some water so I could swallow it better.

I slept without any dreams.

Chapter Twenty-four

By morning I was sore all over, which made my throat feel better in comparison. I'd be wearing turtleneck sweaters for a few weeks.

The arm sling was delivered with a note to follow up with my doctor when I got home. Porsche and I opted for breakfast to be delivered to the room. It was a splurge, but I didn't want the attention and stares I would get if we went down to breakfast. I was positive word had spread that I tangled with the killer…and survived. I apparently kicked his butt since the doctor tended his injuries before seeing me last night. I didn't feel very victorious though.

I savored the last of Alpine Sun's food and even stepped out on the balcony to a balmy nine degrees with the sun shining. My breath turned to shimmering tiny crystals in the dry cold. I never understood when visitors would qualify the cold in Colorado with the statement, "but it's a dry cold." Nine degrees, dry or humid, is still freaking cold, and we aren't even going to talk about the negative temperatures the storm had brought. I missed the raccoons, but they were likely back to their dens all snug.

We finally were all packed and in the lobby standing in line to check out. I wore one of Porsche's scarves around my neck to hide the bruises. They looked worse this morning than they felt, but I didn't want to advertise them. I was also reserving talking to reduce irritation and swelling of my larynx and surrounding tissue. I tried to conceal the bruise on my face from Wade's assault with makeup. I had no idea in sunlight how well it would remain covered.

People seemed conflicted in their response to my presence. Some intentionally made eye contact and smiled or nodded. I believed they were relieved the killer was now in custody and heard I was involved in that outcome. Others avoided eye contact as if I was an unpleasant reminder of the violence that intruded into their world. Then there were the people who glared.

Yes, glared at me. I didn't realize what a rabid following Wade Lochran had for his editorials and personal involvement in organizations. Not until I was part of getting him arrested that is. There had been notes slipped under the door throughout the night and this morning, angry notes defending Lochran and blaming Kara Caine or myself.

I told Porsche to turn them all over to Johan to include with the case files. I figured they would keep in touch, at least for a while. Maybe the long distance thing could work, who was I to say? It amazed me how the notes manufactured any scenario, many convoluted, to make

Lochran the victim rather than a calculating killer simply because he represents what they believe in some fashion.

"Good morning Julienne." Came from behind me. I turned to find Justin with his parents. He held a hand up, "don't talk. I know it hurts." That shy smile was out again. Some young girl was going to melt over him, and probably not that long from now. He had a chivalrous side, he found Johan last night to pass my message and insisted on backing him up.

I shook hands with his parents and smiled a lot. "Dear, you're so brave to have fought him." His mother exclaimed, a hand fluttering to her throat. She made it sound like fighting back against an attacker was somehow unusual.

"Thanks for the dance lessons too. I hope to get to use those moves again soon." He blushed. I suspected I had already been replaced in his affections. His cell phone dinged and he was lost to texting.

I got a tap on my shoulder and turned... to look into Mason's eyes.

"Hi, beautiful. I would've been here last night, but some roads hadn't opened yet." He smiled his million-watt charming smile and placed a quick kiss on my cheek. My heart skipped several beats. Just because I doubted we had a real future didn't mean the man didn't make my blood rush.

People were now staring at him and the hum of whispers underscored the entire lobby noise. He glanced around and then looked at me with questions in his eyes.

"Julienne, is this man bothering you?" Justin asked, loud and clear. I heard Porsche snort a laugh.

"Justin, this is my boyfriend..." I croaked and my hand went to my throat.

Mason opened his mouth, probably to ask if I had a bad cold.

But Porsche cut right to the point. She reached around Mason and removed my scarf to reveal the bruises. "Seems she needed a bodyguard herself." Her voice was a scalpel cutting deep.

He reached up and his long fingers grazed my neck. His eyes were flashing lightning bolts.

His voice was low and lethal, "Who did this?"

"The man is already in police custody, while you were gone on *business*, dude." Justin provided. Oh little Justin, don't poke this bear. But I could've kissed him for saying it.

Then Justin shocked me, and likely everybody else in line and some of the people hanging over the upstairs rail watching, too. "Hey, you can't be her boyfriend." He held up his cell phone with a celebrity news photo of Mason with the little starlet he had been protecting. "Unless you're cheating on one of them." Justin's eyes narrowed. The whispers increased in intensity.

Porsche leaned between Mason and me, "And that is the crux of the issue between you two."

Mason looked nervous as he surveyed the crowd. "Can we step into the restaurant and talk?" He said with a tiny hint of pleading. Porsche stayed in line, she was going to pay for the room service and any of her charges. The rest would go on the business card I had provided at check-in.

Kylie escorted us to a small table near the door of Mountain Chalet, her lips pressed tight. I guessed she was providing me with a fast exit if I needed one.

"Kylie, can you fill him in?" My voice was gravel over cement.

"We've had two murders and snowed in the whole time. Because of all the emergencies, the police had several of us, led by Julienne, gathering information and gossip from the guests. Last night she figured out who the killer was and he tried to silence her permanently." She eyed Mason up and down with a hostile look. "We owe her a lot, she caught the guy before everyone checked out and made an arrest harder."

Mason had listened to Kylie but never stopped looking into my eyes. I wanted to lose myself in the fire of his gaze, but I knew he wasn't ready for commitment. If I hadn't gone through all the emotional wrangling the last several days, I likely would've settled for whatever attention he'd give me just to be looked at like that occasionally.

Sitting here, I realized I wanted commitment, but with a man who was ready for me and my life. I may not want children, but I wanted a devoted man to travel the world with me. Maybe that was asking for too much.

Kylie took my order for iced tea to soothe my throat and Mason's for coffee. I glanced out to the lobby and Porsche and Tammy watched, no doubt ready to intervene.

"I'm sorry I wasn't here for you.   Why didn't you tell me there were murders? I would've found a way to get here." His voice was tender and heavy with concern.

I shook my head no and tried whispering since it wasn't as painful, "You couldn't have made it, and then you'd be worrying." The bodyguard job was a problem, but I didn't want him distracted and potentially hurt either.

He started to speak, but I raised my finger to stop him. "I never thought I'd face the killer like that. It just happened that I put the pieces together and he saw it in my eyes. I didn't pursue the killer, really." I sipped the tea and it soothed as it flowed down my throat.

"Okay, but what else is going on? I know you're upset over my working the bodyguard job." So, he got at least that much.

"You heard what the boy said. To everybody else, you have a girlfriend – whoever hires you as a bodyguard is known as your girl – not me." I took a deep breath, this next part was the hardest. I wanted to say that Brendon would never let anybody think he was with another, but I wouldn't throw an old boyfriend in his face. I had even thought of telling him maybe I needed to hire him, but that would be a low blow. He started to speak, and I held up my hand.

"You promised me you weren't a player anymore. You promised you wanted a serious relationship. I wanted it with you. I like you a lot and it could be more. I'm ready for that, and I want that. I don't think you're actually ready for everything that requires. If you're okay with posing as somebody else's boyfriend, even for a job, then I don't think you really want a serious commitment." I stood up to leave.

"Wait, I want you, I want us. Really I do. Don't overreact about a job." He rushed out the words, not realizing how they sounded. But that meant they were probably a true reflection of how he felt.

I was "overreacting" in his eyes, but would he feel the same way if the roles were reversed and I was publicly linked with another man?

"I think you like the idea of a steady girlfriend, so long as you don't have to alter anything in your life. But that isn't how committed relationships work."

"I know I've been busy. It won't always be this way." He answered. I felt like he wasn't hearing what I was actually saying. Sadly, this is exactly how it would probably remain going forward, maybe a spell of time together. But I now knew I wanted more.

"You really need to look at your life and see if you're ready for the change a devoted and committed relationship will require. Goodbye Mason. Let me know when you're ready for a genuine relationship."

This time I walked out. I joined Porsche who drowned out Mason's parting words with her questions of what did I say and how did he take the news.

If I had known what would happen at this conference, some prescient warning, would I have stayed far away? If I'm honest, I think I would have stayed home.

Thank you for reading!

Dear Reader,

I hope you enjoyed NAILED: Resort to Murder Mystery #2. I really enjoyed writing the characters of Julienne, Porsche, Mason, and the rest of the gang! I hope you enjoyed reading about their adventures, and hope you are looking forward to the next book, SPIKED.

Finally, I need to ask you a favor. If you're so inclined, I'd love a review of NAILED. Whether you loved it or hated it - I'd just enjoy your feedback. Reviews can be tough to come by these days. You, the reader, have the power now to make or break a book.

Also, feel free to contact me at mysterysuspense1@gmail.com if you have spotted any typos that have escaped my proofreader's attention. Subscribe to newsletter for Book Club Discussion Questions: http://eepurl.com/c2DgfT

Thank you for reading NAILED and spending time with me.

In gratitude,

ABOUT THE AUTHOR

Avery Daniels was born and raised in Colorado, graduated from college with a degree in business administration, and has worked in Fortune-500 companies and Department of Defense her entire life. Her most eventful job was apartment management for 352 units. She still resides in Colorado with two brother black cats as her spirited companions. She enjoys scrapbooking and card making, photography, and painting in watercolor and acrylic. She inherited a love for reading from her mother and grandmother and grew up talking about books at the dinner table.

Signup for exclusives http://eepurl.com/c2DgfT
Website: www.Avery-Daniels.com
Goodreads: www.goodreads.com/Avery-Daniels
Facebook: facebook.com/AveryDanielsAuthor
Instgram: instagram.com/avery_daniels1

Next in the Resort to Murder Mystery series is Spiked